Neapolitan Murder

A SPIES AND FOOD TRUCK COZY MYSTERY BOOK 6

ROSIE A. POINT

Neapolitan Murder

A Spies and Food Trucks Cozy Mystery Book 6

Copyright © 2024 by Rosie A. Point

www.rosiepointbooks.com

All Rights Reserved. This publication or parts thereof may not be reproduced in any form, stored, distributed, or transmitted in any form—electronic, mechanical, photocopy, recording or otherwise—except in the case of brief quotations for review purposes.

This is a work of fiction. Any resemblance to actual persons alive or deceased, places, or events is coincidental.

You're invited!

Hi there, reader!

I'd like to formally invite you to join my awesome community of readers. We love to chat about cozy mysteries, cooking, and pets.

It's super fun because I get to share chapters from yet-to-be-released books, fun recipes, pictures, and do giveaways with the people who enjoy my stories the most.

So whether you're a new reader or you've been enjoying my stories for a while, you can catch up with other like-minded readers, and get lots of cool content by visiting my website at *www.rosiepointbooks.com* and signing up for my mailing list.

Or simply search for me on *www.bookbub.com* and follow me there.

I look forward to getting to know you better.

Let's get into the story!

Yours,
Rosie

One

"I HAVE TO TELL YOU SOMETHING." THE WOMAN'S words were a whisper, and she leaned in, grasping the cone of Neapolitan ice cream in pale fingers tipped with crimson nails. "But we can't talk here. It has to be in secret."

I frowned.

Beside me, Smulder was preoccupied serving customers out of the side of the I Scream for Ice Cream truck, his frilly apron doing nothing to reduce the sharp set of his jaw or masculine aura. It would have been comical if I wasn't currently feeling awkward about our "relationship." If it could be classed as a "relationship."

"It's important," the woman, a redhead with freckles across her forehead and sparkling green eyes that were full of mischief, continued. "If you want to keep running your business, you should meet me under the trees near the lake beside the Tickleton Observatory. In ten minutes." And then she shoved five dollars into the plastic tip jar on the counter and walked off.

I took a mental image of her for later dissection.

Now what?

It had been a tough couple of weeks.

Bark, Smulder and I had arrived in Hentie's home town, Tickle, Texas, a couple of weeks ago, only to discover that her dear husband, Franklin, had passed away. Hentie had been so relieved to see us, she'd burst into tears, and what had followed was a period of grief and anger, of trying to make sense of the world, while my boss, Special Agent in Charge Grant, chewed me out every chance he got.

Or that was how it felt anyway.

I needed a break from the mayhem, not more complications.

But curiosity was a killer. I stripped off my apron. "I'll be right back," I said to Smulder. "Watch the truck while I'm gone?"

Smulder hummed under his breath but didn't question me. I'd been taking more breaks from the truck recently, and this time, it wasn't because it was too cold to serve ice cream.

Tickle, Texas—a small town that had a fascinating history, particularly from the prohibition era—was temperate in comparison to the town we'd come from. People still wanted ice cream, and now that we were mere days from Thanksgiving, they were especially keen for pumpkin spice flavors. Soon, peppermint would be all the rage with Christmas on the horizon.

I traipsed down the side steps of the truck, missing Barkington's company. He was back at the house with Hentie, managing her husband's affairs and taking a much-needed break from the truck. She'd already suggested hopping back into the flow of work, but I'd insisted she take the rest.

The truck was parked near Tickle Lake, which was a picturesque green-blue body of water surrounded by woods. Several houses, old and storied, circled the lake, but off to one side, among the trees, was the Tickleton Observatory. It had a domed glass roof and was often empty, but had recently been repainted a brilliant white.

I walked toward it, my feet crunching through the grass then over the dirt road that snaked between the trees. I passed a group of rowdy teenagers, chatting and laughing as they headed toward the ice cream truck, wearing their fall coats, and nudging each other.

The lake was popular, and the locals we'd encountered so far were kind, but weirdly reserved. I'd noticed shifty-eyed behavior on occasion and a lack of conversation.

Oh, there were pleasantries, sure, but the general vibe was that people kept to themselves. Not in keeping with the southern hospitality I'd expected when we'd arrived.

The observatory was flanked by a chain link fence, and I considered it, my fists on my hips. I wasn't about to break and enter without reason. Just because I had the skills of a spy, didn't mean I had to put them to use.

I scanned the fence and the trees.

Ah. There she is.

The woman, her siren red hair tied up in a high pony-tail that fountained atop her head, stood underneath the trees, tapping away on her phone while she waited for me.

I walked up behind her. "You wanted to talk to me about my business?"

The woman shrieked, the sound traveling across the water. She turned toward me. "Where did you come from?" She pressed her phone to her chest.

I had to stop doing that. It was a habit to be as silent as possible, and it made me seem suspicious.

"The ice cream truck," I said, and then I presented my hand with a smile. "April Waters." I used my code name. No one except Smulder knew that my real name was Delta Mission, of the infamous Texas Missions.

Hopefully, I'll get to visit Gamma and Charlie while I'm in Texas.

The woman squeezed my hand once then let it go and wiped her palm off on her blue jeans. She was in her twenties, attractive, with an impish smile. "Hadley McCulloch," she said. "You might have heard of me."

"Heard of you?"

"Oh, sure," she said. "My family's infamous in these parts. The McCullochs used to be moonshiners back in the day." She gave me another of those mischievous grins. "And I'm proud of it. Troublemakers, rabble rousers, you name it. We did it all."

I laughed. "Good to know. But why do you want to talk to me?"

"Because there's trouble brewing," she said, tucking her phone into her jeans. "And not the fun kind."

I raised an eyebrow.

"There's a rumor going around town that a member of the Tickle Ethics Committee has a problem with how you're running your business," Hadley said, with a shrug.

"I don't see why they'd have a problem with the ice cream truck. We applied for the permits and received them. We're allowed to sell our ice cream."

"Yeah, that's not the problem," she said. "Y'all might have the right permits, but this town... It's not what you think it is. It's not what it used to be. Tickle used to be a fun place to live. Parties and celebrations. People coming from far and wide to participate in balls and events, but now? Let's just say that the local government has come down on anyone and anything who 'threatens the peace' of the residents."

"What does that even mean?" I asked.

"That's for them to decide," Hadley said, ominously, and cast her gaze across the water.

I followed her line of sight. A double story wooden house sat between the trees, its darkened windows looking out over the water like wary eyes.

"There's a meeting in the town hall tonight," Hadley said. "I heard a rumor that there's going to be a discussion about your truck. It's at six. Be there if you want to make sure that whoever is working against you doesn't get the last say." And then she gave me a quick nod and walked off. She stopped, resting her palm against a rough-barked trunk. "Oh, and we never talked. Got it?"

"Sure," I said.

And then she hurried off, her steps crunching over grass. She didn't head back toward the dirt road. She kept in line with it instead, like she didn't want to be seen or she suspected someone of watching her.

What a strange town, and an even weirder encounter.

I had more important things to concern myself with

than the town's history. Like maintaining my cover or making sure that Hentie was managing during her time of grief.

But the truck? And serving ice cream to the locals? That definitely made the list of chief worries.

If I couldn't serve ice cream, my cover was no use. And Special Agent in Charge Grant was so far up my butt at the moment, it was a miracle he didn't pop out of my mouth every time I opened it.

I'd have to deal with this committee member's complaints tonight.

I stood beneath a Cottonwood tree, taking in the sounds of nature, the silence from the observatory on the other side of the fence, and—

Movement on the other side of the lake, near that ghastly dark house, caught my attention.

A figure, outfitted in dark clothing, sneaked between the trees, hunched over, clearly trying to avoid notice. They stopped often, peeking out from behind trunks, fixated on the house.

I tilted my head, taking mental images of them as they went.

The person tried to climb the tree they'd been hiding behind, grabbing at the bottom branches, and scrambling to pull themselves up. The bough snapped, the sharp sound followed by a thump as the dark clad figure was deposited onto the ground. They rose and ran off, disappearing into the forest that flanked the house.

Not what I'd expected when I'd arrived in Tickle.

But then, what was life without a little mystery and intrigue?

Two

That evening...

"I'll be back at the house by seven, hopefully," I said, pinning the phone to my ear as I got out of my food truck.

I'd parked it down the long broad street that led toward the town hall. Already, folks had parked their cars along it, and people walked down the paved sidewalks. Apparently, these meetings were important in Tickle.

"Okay, lekker," Hentie said. "Listen, are you sure you want to go to the meeting, April? Every time I used to go, it would always end up annoying me. They like to talk about silly stuff that doesn't matter."

"This is for the truck," I said. "I won't be long. Do you need me to come back early?" I wanted to support Hentie during her grieving period. Her husband had traveled a lot, so Hentie had decided to go on cruises when she could, and they'd spent a large portion of their time in different cities across the country, but this was their home base. There had to be memories here. Memories that Hentie might want to avoid.

"Ag nee, man. I'll be fine," Hentie said. "I've got my Blaffies, and Oliver is home as well." Oliver was Smulder's code name, not that Hentie knew it. "Besides, I've got the party to finish planning. I want it to be a celebration of Franklin's life, and there's lots of things to organize."

"I'll be home soon. Call me if you need anything."

"Ek sal. I will." And then she hung up.

I tucked my phone into my purse, strung it over my shoulder then locked the ice cream truck and headed toward the town hall. Smulder had opted out of joining me for the meeting and had decided to take a leisurely stroll along the lakefront before heading back to Hentie's mansion. Technically, it was her husband's mansion, but everything belonged to Hentie now.

Crickets chirped in the gathering quiet, but the town hall, a brick building with a pretty white clock tower, had its doors open, light spilling onto the steps. The hubbub of people talking inside came with it.

I entered and found that most of the seats were taken —long wooden benches had been set out and everyone was talking.

They silenced the minute I stepped through the doors.

I spotted redheaded Hadley off to the side, leaning against the wall, her arms folded. She didn't acknowledge me, but averted her eyes.

Slowly, the chatter started back up.

Great. More attention. I didn't need trouble in this town. We'd moved on from three towns when the poop had hit the fan, and I wanted to stay here for as long as it took to get Hentie on her feet and happy.

And then what? Leave her here?

I wasn't sure what the future would hold, and I didn't want to leave Hentie or Barkington behind. I practiced my breathing, four breaths in, hold for four counts, four breaths out, then slipped into a spot at the end of a bench near the back of the hall.

The woman beside me gave me a tight smile and shifted over so I could get more comfortable.

"Thanks," I said.

She didn't say anything back, but gave a nod before continuing her conversation with the guy next to her.

I couldn't fault these people for not falling over themselves to welcome me. Heck, I had no idea what kind of strangeness was happening in this town, but I was intrigued. The interior of the hall was friendly, with pictures of the town framed along brick walls and wooden floors that creaked, a central light fixture that looked as old as the building itself and cast warm, buttery light over the benches.

Another five or so minutes later, a woman in a neat cream blouse and a navy blue pencil skirt took to the stage. Her dark eyes roved over the crowd as she took her place behind a pulpit. The gathered townsfolk quieted.

"Good evening, ladies and gentlemen," she said. "I'm glad you could make it for tonight's town hall. We've got a few items on the agenda, but—"

"Mayor Barrera!" A woman's hand shot up in the front row. Sans a ring, nails immaculately short and unpainted.

"We'll get to your issue shortly, Miss Dawson," the mayor said, pursing her lips, her eyes narrowing a little. "Let's get through the initial welcome before we begin."

Miss Dawson dropped her hand into her lap. I couldn't make out her face from where I was seated, but she had long dark, glossy hair identical to the woman beside her. While she sat stiff and upright, the other dark-haired lady slouched, head lowered.

I took an image of them and filed it away. Silly. I had an eidetic memory, so I could go through these stills later, but there was no reason to specifically take snapshots of these women or this town. Old habits died hard.

The mayor, tucking caramel brown hair behind her ear, gave her welcome. "We've gathered on short notice to discuss some last minute changes to the Thanksgiving Parade this coming Thursday, as well as a few other issues that were brought up by the Tickle Ethics Committee. First let me say that our town has been doing amazingly over the past months. I've heard from my friends at Travel Texas that they're impressed by how peaceful Tickle has become."

Miss Dawson's hand shot up again and waggled in the air, but Mayor Barrera ignored her.

"Usually, I'd assemble a panel to discuss the parade, but since this is a last minute thing, we really didn't have the time," the Mayor said. "Now, usually we start the parade at nine in the morning and have the floats lined up and ready to go by then. This year, we hoped to livestream the event to ViewTube, but our camera crew has had trouble getting here by that time. I'm moving to shift the parade to noon."

Gasps moved through the hall.

"I'd like to open this to discussion and invite comments," Mayor Barrera said, tapping her fingers on the wooden pulpit. "Please raise your hand if you have input to offer."

Miss Dawson's hand waved frantically in the front row. The dark-haired woman beside her sank even lower.

"I'm only taking comments about the Thanksgiving parade at this time," the Mayor said, pointedly.

A man in the middle of the room put up his hand.

"Yes, Roger? Go ahead."

"Thank you, Mayor," he said. "I have a concern about the parade taking place that late. Most of us planned to be home by two in the afternoon to spend time with our families."

"I have two cousins coming down from Washington," a woman called out near the back.

"One at a time please, Tillie," Mayor Barrera said. "Please continue, Roger."

"If we host the parade at noon, we'll only be done by four in the afternoon," Roger said, running a liver-spotted hand over his gray hair. "My grandkids are here for Thanksgiving. I don't want to spend the afternoon driving the mermaid float only to—"

"There shouldn't even *be* a mermaid float." That came from Miss Dawson, who had dropped her hand and risen from her seat, turning to face Roger. She was a striking woman. Rosebud red lips. Probably around my age—in her thirties—and with a mole beside her mouth. She reminded me of a modern day Scarlett O'Hara, and she had the dramatic movements to match. "That float is an abomination."

"Victoria, sit down," Mayor Barrera said. "We've already spoken on the mermaid float and decided it would go ahead. It's for the kids."

"It doesn't even make sense," Victoria Dawson said, snapping her blue eyed gaze to the front. "If it were up to me, there would be no mermaid float at all."

"You would say that," Hadley put in, rolling her eyes heavenward. "We worked darn hard on that float. We're not going to—"

"Enough," Mayor Barrera called.

But the arguments had already broken out.

"I came here because I'm the head of the Tickle Ethics Committee," Victoria Dawson said. "That's got to mean something in this town. And I'm telling you, this place is getting out of hand. First the mermaid float, and now there are strangers serving ice cream in town. Who knows what kind of... *unnatural* things they might be putting in the dairy. I saw a group of teenagers heading out there today. We don't need our young ones corrupted by strangers."

"What, like sugar?" Roger asked, snorting.

"No. Like drugs. Or alcohol."

"Yeah, you would be worried about that, wouldn't you?" Hadley called out.

"What exactly do you mean by that?" Victoria yelled back at her. "How dare you talk to me like that given *your* family history. Moonshiner."

Hisses and gasps traveled through the room.

"You're out of your mind," Hadley said. "That's ancient history."

Mayor Barrera slapped her hand down on the pulpit, hard. The crowd quieted. "That's enough," she said. "We'll take a vote on when we'll start the parade on Thanksgiving day and be done with the issue. As for the ice cream truck, there's no indication that the owners are going to harm the town. This is not a witch hunt, and Tickle needs tourism and newcomers. This is going to be the best tourism spot in Texas. The perfect family vacation destination."

Victoria jumped out of her seat again. "My house was broken into this afternoon."

Another round of shocked responses and intakes of breath.

"My suggestion is that you talk to Sheriff Remington and his deputies about that," Mayor Barrera said. "We—"

"A very important family heirloom was stolen," Victoria continued. "You can't tell me this has nothing to do with the newcomers or the... the sheer unsavory behavior of the tourists who are coming for this parade. I demand—"

"Enough, Victoria," Mayor Barrera said.

Tension rippled through the room.

"I'm sorry your home was broken into, but you'll need to talk to local law enforcement about the theft. They'll help you. As for the ice cream, the truck owner has a permit and they're abiding by the law. There's nothing that can be done about that."

Victoria glared at the mayor, grinding her teeth. "We'll just see about that, won't we?" And then she clicked her fingers at the women beside her. "Come, sister," she said.

The pair walked out of the town hall together, the sister with her head bowed, pretty blue eyes darting left and right, and Victoria with her chin high, nose in the air.

Mayor Barrera released a breath once they were gone. "Now that we can have a civilized vote, let's see a show of hands for a noon day parade."

The tension eased in the room now that Victoria was gone.

But my spy senses told me this wasn't the end of trouble in Tickle.

Three

The following night...

HENTIE'S HOUSE HAD A HISTORY. A THREE-story brick mansion with a tower, it was more like a castle than a mansion, and it reminded me a lot of the Gossip Inn, with its nooks and crannies, thick wood doors and squeaking staircase. A massive painted picture of Hentie and her husband dominated the space over the mantelpiece—the pair smiling, Barkington seated in Hentie's lap, his Chihuahua face turned toward his owner.

Tonight, music drifted through the living room accompanied by bursts of laughter and the hum of conversation. Most of the town had turned up for Hentie's celebration of Franklin's life, and she was happy about it.

Hentie, my best friend, stood beside a photograph of Franklin, positioned carefully on an easel and draped with flowers, talking to the party guests and sipping from a champagne glass. Barkington was tucked into her arms, snoozing, and occasionally opening an eye to assess the guests who dared interrupt his nap time.

"She looks content," Smulder said.

He'd approached from the left—the open archway that led into the gleaming, tiled kitchen.

"Content is the right word," I said. "It sounds terrible, but I'm glad that Franklin didn't suffer for long. And that Hentie didn't either. It's awful to watch someone you care about in pain." My gaze darted left to where Brian stood in a well-fitted suit. His dark hair was parted and combed tonight, and he looked different. Older, even. More mature.

Possibly, that was because of what I'd put him through.

"Have you heard from Grandpa?" I asked, using the code name for Special Agent in Charge Grant.

"No," he said. "Not today. But I'm due for a call with him."

"Are you? He's been calling me almost every day to check that we're behaving as expected."

"That *we're* behaving as expected?" Smulder asked.

"I don't like your tone," I sniffed, with a hint of a smile.

Hentie twiddled her fingers in our direction. It was so good to be in her presence again. I'd missed her terribly when she'd left the food truck. Tonight, she'd chosen a black pantsuit, with a matching black shirt underneath. If not for her bobbly gray bun, she would've reminded me of Johnny Cash.

"Excuse me," Smulder said, and walked off, taking his cologne and the air in the room with him.

I walked toward Hentie and found her chatting to Hadley, the redhead from the town hall meeting. "—sure the mayor will join us."

"Ag, no," Hentie said. "There's no way she'll come here. You know what these people are like. They don't want to be seen as too fun or loose."

"It's good to let loose once in a while," Hadley said, then gave me a quick smile. "Didn't expect to see you here, April."

"I'm good friends with Hentie," I replied. "She usually works on the ice cream truck with me."

Hadley's eyes flashed with excitement. "That's cool. You know, I've always wanted to do something like that. Travel around the country. Meet new people. But I like Tickle too much. It's got the right *vibes*, you know?" She hesitated. "Unless you count the vibes that Victoria gives off."

"She was outspoken at the town meeting."

Hentie leaned in. I'd told her about the meeting and how it would affect the truck—it wouldn't, given that the mayor had shut down Victoria's complaints.

Hadley waved a hand. "Don't take it personally. She's always complaining about one thing or the other. She's got this obsession with keeping the town clean."

"Yeah, you mentioned that."

Hadley nodded. "Tickle was packed full of moonshiners back during the prohibition era. That's the reason the town is named Tickle in the first place."

"Because they were dronk?" Hentie asked. "Drunk." She clarified.

"Probably," Hadley laughed. "They made some strong stuff. The town was initially separated into two groups of people. The moonshiners, who desperately wanted to have fun, make a living, and who didn't want to be controlled by the government. And then there were people like Victoria Dawson and her sister, Emery."

Ah. Emery Dawson. My mind flashed back to the image of the pair leaving the town hall, Emery with her head bowed, wearing black.

Black like the person who'd been sneaking around in

the woods outside that house. Could that have been the Dawson house?

"The Dawsons hate anything to do with drinking or partying or fun. Even non-alcoholic fun. As you could probably tell by the town hall meeting. Victoria doesn't even want us to do the Thanksgiving Day parade on Thursday. I don't get it, personally. She's kooky beans." Hadley shrugged. "They were one of the original families."

"This is like a movie or something," Hentie said. "The prohibition and the founding families."

"You don't have stories like that where you're from, Hentie?" Hadley asked.

Hentie nearly choked on her champagne, and Barkington gave a yap of protest at the interruption in his nap. "Oh no, we have much worse stories than that. My country has an unfortunate history."

"Most countries do," I said. "It's important to treat each other with respect, so we can make a better—"

A thump sounded from the foyer, followed by a creak and a slam, loud enough to be audible over the music pumping through the speakers.

"What was that?" Hadley asked, spinning toward the archway that led into the room.

A woman appeared in the doorway to the living room, her fists clenched at her sides, and her hair dripping wet. Weird since there wasn't any rain tonight.

Victoria Dawson, sopping wet, sploodged across the room toward the stereo. She shut off the speaker, glaring around at the gathered men and women.

I took a mental snapshot of the moment out of reflex.

"You," she said, pointing a finger at Hentie. "You are in contravention of the Tickle Ethics Committee's law about parties after eleven at night."

"Boohockey," said a man nearby. He was diminutive and had chosen to wear a bright purple ascot that clashed with a red shirt. His dark hair stuck up on his head in spikes—like he'd stuck a fork in a wall socket and paid the ultimate price.

"You shut your mouth, Dunnels," Victoria said, and switched her gaze back to Hentie. She squidged closer, dripping water on the persian rug. "You left your sprinkler system on after hours and you're throwing a raucous party. I demand you shut it down."

Barkington growled, patting his paws against Hentie's forearm.

Hentie tilted her head. "Or what? What you gonna do, huh?"

Victoria, who was much younger than Hentie, took a single moist step backward. "I'll— Uh, I'll call the cops."

"So do it then," she said. "This is my husband's memorial. And the whole town knows about it. Sheriff Remington is right there." Hentie pointed to the sheriff, who had a hors d'oeuvre halfway to his mouth. He gave an awkward wave.

Victoria growled under her breath. "You'll pay for this," she whispered. "You'll all pay." She swung a pointed finger around the room, singling out a few people, before storming off toward the exit.

One of the guests switched on the stereo again.

"That's her favorite line," Hadley said, then held up a fist and waggled it. "You'll all pay." She'd done a pretty good impression of Victoria's squeaky voice. "Good job not letting her bully you into backing down."

Hentie pet Barkington's caramel-colored ears. "She doesn't scare me."

"She's been trying to shut down my float idea ever since I came up with it," Hadley said. "Who knew mermaids would be such a personal affront to her? Say, y'all should come by the carnival grounds tomorrow. We're using the space as a set up area for the parade. Come see what we've made. I bet everyone will want to take a break and have an ice cream."

"That's a great idea," I said, and glanced toward the exit.

Victoria was gone, but the uneasy feeling she'd brought into the room remained.

<h1 style="text-align:center">Four</h1>

THE FOLLOWING MORNING, AS BRIGHT AND EARLY as we could manage after the party, Hentie, Bark, and I got onto the ice cream truck, our minds set on the carnival grounds and the floats. I was excited to check out what the townsfolk had created, and Hentie needed a distraction now that Franklin's memorial was over.

The solicitor had called Hentie to talk about his will, but she hadn't yet had him over to discuss what Franklin had left to whom. He had estranged children and had often talked about donating money to charities he deemed worthy.

The more I learned about Franklin, the more intrigued I became. He was an enigma. I'd heard him talking to Hentie via Zoom chat, but I'd never been introduced.

After Hentie had strapped Sir Barkington the Blaf into

his crate and clipped on her seatbelt, I started the engine and started down the long road that led between the trees.

Hentie's mansion was attached to the lake, but the property was huge, and the gates were a five minute drive from the house. The neighbors weren't close by either.

"Oliver doesn't want to come with us today?" Hentie asked.

"He's resting," I said. "Or exploring Tickle. I'm not sure which."

"Huh."

"What?"

"You guys are still pretending you're not in love with each other?"

"Love!" My foot jolted down on the brake pedal, and Hentie squawked at the sudden stop. "Sorry," I managed. "Just didn't expect you to, uh, put it like that." Love was not what this was. It was attraction, sure. But love? No way, no how. Not after Mickey.

"If you say so, April," Hentie said. "But come on. You two can't keep your eyes off each other."

"My eyes are firmly focused on the road."

Thankfully, Hentie let the topic rest. We drove past the wrought iron gates, flung open after last night's guests had left. Tickle was a safe town, barring stolen heirlooms, apparently, and most people didn't lock their doors.

Hentie was the exception. She locked everything.

When I'd asked her about it, she'd spun me a tale about her South African roots and crimes of opportunity.

The ice cream truck bumped over the dirt road as we rounded the lake. We passed by several houses. One of them stood out to me—its dark front facing the road, the back looking out on the lake. This was the house directly across from the observatory. The one where I'd spotted that dark figure.

"Who lives here?" I asked.

"I believe it's the Dawson's house," Hentie said.

Ah. "You live this close to Victoria?"

"Ja. But she's not a problem for me. Or she wasn't because I haven't been around, and neither has Franklin. He's usually working, and I've been on cruises and with you."

I smiled. I'd never forget the circumstances under which we'd met. It amazed me how far we'd come together as friends. Especially now that Hentie knew I was on the run. She wasn't privy to the details, but she understood that I needed to keep my nose clean.

Fifteen minutes later, we parked outside the carnival grounds—two fields adjacent to each other, with plenty of cars parked on the grass outside the fence. The ground near the gates had been trampled to dirt, but the fields were green and lush.

Across them, floats were being constructed, with the

sounds of frantic hammering and talking traveling through the wind whipped grass.

"Wow," Hentie said. "Ek is opgewonde! I'm excited. Can you believe this? Look there, a float with a giant turkey on the back."

We grabbed Bark from his crate and then started past the fence, taking our time wandering past floats with bursts of color. One float was covered in paper flowers in blues, reds, and whites. Another was made to look like a stage, with hay bales piled either side of it and a seat up top. A live musician, perhaps? Another float had a giant pickle attached, floating this way and that, wearing a cowboy hat and a mustache.

"This is so fun!" Hentie said, holding Barkington close. "Look, there's one with Father Christmas."

"Father Christmas?"

"That's what we call him. You call him Santa Claus," Hentie said.

I pointed at the mermaid float nearby. It depicted a beautiful dark-skinned mermaid cresting a rock, colorful purple hair cascading down her back. She wore a pearly pink seashell bra and had a bright green tail, a comical look of excitement on her face. One eye had been painted on slightly skew.

"We have to fix this." Hadley had her hands on her hips as she lectured a teenage girl whose overalls were splattered with paint. "She looks like a goofball with the skew eye."

"Sorry," the teen said. "I tried, but I guess I didn't step back to get perspective."

"I don't care, Latisha," Hadley said. "Fix it. We can't have a goofy looking mermaid in the parade. Victoria will never let me hear the end of it."

"I'm on it." The teen hurried off, joined by one of her friends, and the pair clambered onto the float together.

Hadley waved us over. "You came," she said, whipping out her phone. "Good. We need all hands on deck for this. Take my number in case we need more help later."

"Jinne jong," Hentie said. "I like decorating as much as the next woman, but I didn't sign up for this."

"We came bearing ice cream, if that helps," I said, but we exchanged numbers regardless. It was good to connect with the locals, and she *had* warned me about Victoria's attempts to bring down the truck.

"True." Hadley pointed that crimson nail at me then tossed her long red ponytail over her shoulder. She had a few splatters and splodges of paint on her face, but nothing that marred her prettiness. "So? What do you guys think? Apart from the kooky beans expression."

"She's beautiful," Hentie said.

I agreed. Even Barkington gave a bark of approval.

"See? I don't get why Victoria is so hurt about it."

Hadley waved a hand. "Nevermind. It's not like she can stop the parade now. It's happening at nine on Thursday, no matter what she wants."

The clamor in the field, the talking and hard work, was comforting, and my concerns about Victoria had faded overnight. Every town had a troublemaker and a stickler for the rules. It seemed both had overlapped in Victoria Dawson.

The three of us stood admiring the float, Bark occasionally snuffling at Hentie's arms.

"Excuse me." A man appeared from around the side of the mermaid's tail, and I recognized him from the party last night. He was the guy with the tufts of hair. Today, he'd chosen a white ascot that was now colored with paint, and a pair of blue jean overalls.

"Dale," Hadley said. "Are you lost? The turkey float is near the entrance."

"I was actually hoping to talk to you, Miss McCulloch," he said, clapping thick-fingered hands together and squeezing. "About Victoria."

"I'm not interested." Hadley walked off and left Dale, or "Dunnels" as Victoria had called him, standing beside the mermaid tail wringing his hands.

"She's stressed," I said, by way of excuse.

"The mermaid's eye is skew." Hentie pointed at it.

Dale came forward, his gait uneven, and stood beside

us. Barkington gave a low growl, but he didn't come too close to Hentie or the Chihuahua. "Told her she should paint it on herself," Dale sighed. "You haven't seen Victoria?"

"No," I said.

Hentie shook her head.

"Why?"

"Just that she said she would come by the turkey float this morning," he replied. "I've been meaning to talk to her about some intensely private matters." He pressed his thin lips together and outward, as if we'd asked *him* about what those matters were.

"Haven't seen her, sorry."

Dale grumbled under his breath and wandered off.

A minute later, Hadley popped her head around the side of the mermaid float, holding two paint brushes. "Is he gone?"

I nodded.

"Y'all better bring me some ice creams or start painting," Hadley said briskly. "We're on the clock. T-minus three days until the parade. Come on, people, this mermaid's eye isn't going to fix itself!"

<h1 style="text-align:center">Five</h1>

That afternoon, Hentie, Bark and I returned to the mansion together, having avoided painting floats but having made loads of ice cream sales. We'd saved the last bit of Neapolitan ice cream for ourselves, and we ate it out of two cups, decorated with the pink and blue colors of the I Scream for Ice Cream truck, as we walked up the porch steps.

The weather was cool, but not unpleasant, and the sweet ice cream helped soothe me after a long day on my feet.

"I can't believe it's almost Thanksgiving," I said.

"I'm excited," Hentie said. "It's only going to be my third ever Thanksgiving." She gave a smile, but her bottom lip trembled. She put on a brave face. I'd heard her crying last night before bed in her room upstairs. She missed Franklin, and this had to be tough on her.

I reached out and squeezed her shoulder.

Hentie gave a shake of her head. "I think I need to go lie down for a while," she said. "Can you watch Barkington for me?"

"Of course." I took Bark from her arms, and he gave me happy licks on the chin.

We entered the house together, and Hentie took the stairs to the second floor. I stayed downstairs, entered the living room—clean after the party thanks to the helpful cleaning service that had come by this morning—and sat down in a wingback armchair.

The room had an almost regal aesthetic, with a grandfather clock tick-tocking in the corner. It was four in the afternoon. Not too late to head out and explore Tickle, but after our visit to the carnival grounds, I was pooped.

I yawned and rested my head against the chair. Bark let out a yip—a request to be let down, and I set him on the Persian rug, where he immediately scratched behind his ear, then sniffed at a dark spot. Water from where Victoria had been standing last night?

My eyes drifted shut but my phone buzzed in my pocket before I could get any rest.

Only three people had this number.

Smulder.

Hentie.

Special Agent in Charge Grant.

I didn't need to guess who it was this time. "Hello, Grandpa," I answered. "How are you?"

"How do you think I am?" Grant snarled down the line.

"I'd imagine you've gone through your blood pressure meds for the day," I said. "I hope you've been taking your multivitamins as well, Gramps. Might want to start meditating routinely."

"That's hilarious, April," Grant said. "I'd say start a comedy tour, but given the current circumstances, that wouldn't be wise, would it? Then again, at this rate, you might as well start screaming your name and address at passersby."

"That seems excessive."

"Don't talk to *me* about excessive, April."

"Grandpa, everything's fine," I said. "I haven't run into any trouble in Texas, yet."

"Let's keep it that way," Grant said. "Because I've been hearing some interesting rumors around the house." Chatter in the NSIB headquarters?

"About what, Gramps?"

"About there being some unwelcome friends in Texas," he said. "Looking for a particular family."

My family. The Missions.

"You're sure about that?"

"No," he said. "But I've had friends and distant relations reach out to let me know that this is a particularly dangerous time for the Waters family."

"Ah," I said. "I can assure you that the Waters family is fine."

"You're in contact with your relatives?" Grant asked, sounding like he was about to blow the top off his skull.

"No," I said. "I haven't. But I'm confident in my family's ability to look after themselves."

"Maybe too confident," Grant said. "That's why you're in trouble."

I couldn't respond to that without sounding snarky, and I'd learned that snark wasn't appreciated by my superiors, or anyone, really. "Grandpa, I promise you, I'm behaving. I'm not going to slip up."

"I trust that Oliver is keeping you safe," he said.

"Yes. He's doing everything he can to make sure my life is as pedestrian as possible."

A grunt of approval. "Keep your head down. We don't want unwanted guests sniffing you out. The minute the coast is clear, you can move on from that town. Stay out of trouble. I'll talk to you again soon."

"Can't wait," I said drily, but he'd already hung up.

I didn't blame my boss for being frustrated with me, but it wasn't like I'd gone looking for trouble. I'd just stumbled into a whole mess of it over the past few months. From the cruise ship murder, to the graveyard catastrophe, and, most recently, the arson at the guesthouse. Was it my fault that trouble followed me wherever I went?

Human nature was a funny thing.

People could be kind and caring, giving and willing to help. Or they could be murderous and selfish. Sometimes, I struggled to find the in between, after everything I'd witnessed through my years working for the Crown Prince of Dubai.

Barkington gave a tiny ruff.

And I smiled at him. At least, he was simple and sweet. Never gave any trouble apart from a few barking fits here or there.

"I love you, Bark," I said.

He whined and pawed at the wet carpet.

"Don't do that. You'll ruin that rug. Not that it's not already ruined after Victoria got water all over it."

Another whine, but Barkington didn't keep digging.

I lifted my phone and tapped through to my messages and opened my text conversation with Smulder.

> Grandpa says there are some unwelcome friends in Texas, looking for the Waters family.

> Thanks for letting me know.

Usually, I wouldn't tell Smulder anything about Grant's information, mostly because he heard it first hand from Grant himself, but this was important. Something I wanted Smulder to know immediately. If there were criminals or enemy operatives looking for me or my family, we might have to leave sooner rather than later, and I was starting to enjoy Tickle.

I'd hoped we could enjoy Christmas and the New Year here before moving on. Help Hentie get over her grief and—

Barkington barked again. He sniffled the carpet.

"Bark," I said, "No scratching, all right? And keep it down. Hentie's trying to get some shut eye."

But Barkington replied with three yaps in rapid succession.

I reached for him, but instead of pattering into my arms, he ran toward the living room exit.

"Bark? What on earth?" Barkington loved being held. This was the third time Barkington had made a break for it.

The first had been on the cruise ship, when he'd run from a sticky situation. The second, had been when we'd been on a ghost tour in a graveyard. That time, he'd discovered a body.

My stomach turned.

We'd locked the house on our way out. Unless a corpse

had magically appeared in the house, there wasn't a chance this was anything sinister.

Barkington ruffed again.

"Bark! Keep it down," I hissed.

He pitter-pattered back into the living room and barked at me so hard that his tiny doggy body jerked on the spot. And then, he turned around and darted out of sight again.

"All right," I said. "All right, I'm coming."

I followed him into the hall.

Bark waited for me at the base of the stairs. He ran up them and stopped on the landing, waiting for me. The stairs split off to the left and right, leading to the second floor, and he took the right staircase, heading away from Hentie's bedroom and toward mine.

"Where are you taking me, Bark?" I whispered.

He darted to the end of the hall and started scratching at a section of wooden paneling.

Odd.

"What are you doing?" I stopped beside him.

He gave a small ruff and scratched at the skirting board, annoyed about something. I watched him carefully. What about this particular section of wall was bothering him?

I pressed my hand flat against it. The paneling depressed inward. More than it should have.

"Huh." Immediately, I reached up and started feeling around the edges of the paneling. This was an old house. A prohibition era house. It made sense that there would be hidden nooks and crannies. My fingers traveled down, around the outside of the panel and—

I grazed a wooden knob. It was nothing more than a slightly raised section of wood. I pressed on it, and a click reverberated through the panel.

Bark stopped scratching. He tilted his head, giving me a beady-eyed Chihuahua look.

"What did you find?" I picked him up and stepped back, hooking my fingers around the side of the panel and pulling it open.

The answer presented itself to me in the form of a room, illuminated by gaps in wooden boards that had been nailed over a window. And the body of Victoria Dawson, resting in an armchair, her head lolling to the left and her gaze unseeing.

Six

I held Barkington close, studying the scene and taking multiple mental images. Each of those pictures attached to a corkboard in my mind.

"Smulder's going to hate this," I muttered, and glanced over my shoulder at the empty hall. "How did you know, Bark?" I stroked his ears and took a single step into the room.

The room's interior was hexagonal in shape, the floor made of the same wooden boards as the rest of the house, except here, they were worn and looked as if they hadn't been cared for or used in years. Oddly, the floor itself was dust free, but then, there was a broom leaning against the wall to my right.

The murderer had swept the room.

But how had two people, both Victoria, the victim, and the murderer gotten into the room?

This was *not* natural causes. For one, Victoria had been a young, healthy and very much alive woman the last time we'd seen her. For another, whoever had killed her had taken bright red lipstick and drawn three 'x' marks over either of her cheeks.

A cigarette butt lay on the floor near the chair, crushed as if put out on the flooring. And an empty bottle was discarded off to the right.

"Bark," I said. "Stay out here." I put him down and gestured for him to sit.

The Chihuahua whined but did as he was told.

I entered the room and walked over to the bottle. It lay on its side, the label facing upward. Beside it, a syringe with a broken needle. The bottle was empty, but the label was clear.

99.9% ethanol. About 20 milliliters of it.

This amount of ethanol, injected directly into the bloodstream would be fatal, causing nervous system shutdown and even cardiac arrest.

Whoever had done this wanted to be sure that Victoria didn't make it out of the room alive.

But what was with the markings on the cheeks?

They reminded me of something, and I crouched there for a moment, eyes closed, going over the facts in my mind and trying to find the memory I associated with those markings. This death was so specific. The alcohol, the locked room, the cigarette butt, the lipstick markings, and the way that the killer had swept the floor.

How had they found this room?

And how had Victoria gotten in here in the first place?

The windows were boarded up, and this secret room was on the second floor. I couldn't find mention of the symbols in my memory, so my eyes snapped open, searching for more evidence.

Victoria was in the same clothing she'd had on when she'd entered the house last night and interrupted the party. A black hoodie, a pair of jeans. I didn't touch her body—didn't want to meddle with the evidence noticeably—but it looked dry to the touch.

She'd gone out, though. She'd left the mansion.

Did that mean whoever had intercepted her had done so after she'd left? Or had she stayed without Hentie's knowledge?

The party had been fun, the guests celebrated Franklin's life and had stayed late. *And the front gates were open.* Anyone could have entered the property during that time.

I filtered through the facts in rapid succession and kept looking around the room.

Apart from the broom off to one side, and Victoria's body, there was nothing else in here. It wasn't like this space was being used for storage. I had to talk to Hentie about this. And call 911.

This had happened in Hentie's house. After her party. And in a locked room that only she would have known about.

There was a strong chance that Sheriff Remington would blame her for this.

The sheriff was at the party too.

Most of the townsfolk had been there.

The list populated in my mind, along with images of the guests that were attached to the corkboard. Thin red lines spread from the central images of Victoria Dawson's body, to those of the attendees.

Hadley McCulloch was first up—clearly motivated against Victoria. She was the one who had warned me about her plan to get the truck's permit revoked. And she'd clearly despised Victoria, as evidenced by her continuous references to her being "no fun." But was she hateful enough to murder her?

Whoever had done this had taken the murder to the next level.

This was personal.

To poison them in such a specific way, to mark their body, and then to hide them in this room? Why here? Why in a locked room, but do such an obvious calling card by way of the lipstick marks?

"Who else?" I murmured, taking a step out of the room to join Bark, who lay on all fours, a paw pressed over his trembling snout.

The mayor hadn't liked Victoria, and she wasn't at the party that night. Her image attached itself to the corkboard, another thin red line snaking toward the picture of the crime scene.

And then, there was Dale Dunnels, who had both been at the memorial and had come by Hadley's float this morning, asking after the victim.

The thoughts cascaded over me in rapid succession. It felt as if time had slowed, but in reality, mere minutes had passed since I'd unlocked the strange trap door in the wall.

There would be more suspects, but for now, I had to get the cops over here.

I got my phone out of my pocket then hesitated.

Hentie first.

"Bark," I said. "We need to warn Hentie. I need you to stay here and bark if you see anyone come near this room."

The Chihuahua whined and tilted his head.

"Please?"

He gave a cute ruff in response.

"I knew I could count on you." This was a disaster. Both for Hentie, after she'd lost her beloved husband, and for me. Smulder was going to have an aneurysm. Special Agent in Charge Grant would likely descend on this town and drag me into obscurity himself if word of this got out.

Why was it that these things always happened to the people I cared about?

I knocked on Hentie's bedroom door once.

My heart skipped a beat when she didn't immediately answer.

"Hentie?'

"Ja?"

Sweet relief. She was alive. I opened the door and found Hentie rubbing her eyes and sitting up in the king-sized bed, the sheets falling away as she sat up. She was still in her pantsuit. The poor thing had been so emotionally exhausted she'd fallen asleep.

"I have bad news."

Her brow wrinkled.

"I found a body," I said.

"Grap jy? Are you joking? Because that's not funny, April."

"I wish I was kidding around," I said. "Victoria Dawson's body is in a secret room down the hall. Barking-ton's watching the door to make sure nobody goes inside. I needed to tell you before I called 911."

"A secret room?" Hentie scrambled out of bed, tugging her pants straight. "Show me."

I admired her courage. Hentie had been squeamish

over bodies in the past, but she'd likely grown used to encountering them thanks to the sheer amount of murders we'd solved. And that Halloween killing had been particularly gross.

I led Hentie to the open section of wall, and she stopped several paces back from it, her hand flying to her mouth. "Ag nee," she whispered. "You weren't joking. But how—?"

"Did you know there were secret rooms like this in the house?" I asked.

Hentie shook her head, her gray bun bobbling. "No. I mean, it's an old house, so anything's possible, but no, I didn't realize that there were secret rooms. How did you find it?"

"Barkington led me to it."

Hentie took a stumbling step forward, and I caught her arm and steadied her. "Do you need to sit down?"

"No," she said, and swayed on the spot. "I just don't get it. How? How? Why is she even in my house in the first place? And who would do such a terrible thing?"

"Don't worry," I said. "It'll be all right. Sheriff Remington will handle this. There's got to be a simple explanation for how this happened." But I had little faith that any of what I'd said was true.

This was going to cause a lot of trouble, not just for us, but in Tickle itself. I lifted my phone and dialed 911.

Seven

My faith in Sheriff Remington and local law enforcement had dwindled rapidly after they'd arrived on the scene. Not only had the sheriff and his deputies gawked at the body like they'd never seen anything like it before, but Remington had excused himself and gone to the bathroom. The sound of him retching wasn't something I'd forget in a while.

The police had cordoned off the room. They'd called in a local coroner. And they'd faffed around like chickens over a clutch of eggs.

After forty five minutes, I approached Sheriff Remington. "Would you like to take me down to the station and question me?"

Remington, green around the gills, adjusted his belt

over his belly and cleared his throat. "Yeah, that's a good idea. The two of you will have to be taken in for questioning. Let's go."

Hentie grabbed Barkington, and we followed the sheriff down to his cruiser, marked with the Howard County Sheriff's Department badge. We drove to a dingy building in the center of town, flanked by two expanses of yellowing grass and a flag that hung limply against the flagpole.

The interior of the sheriff's department wasn't any better. A sleepy-looking receptionist manned the desk and barely glanced at the sheriff as he entered. Remington strode through a room stacked with desks facing each other and pointed at a deputy sitting behind one.

"Hank," he said. "You're with me."

"What's up, Sheriff?"

"I need you to interview this here, uh, lady." He gestured to Hentie. "About the corpse we just found in her house."

"C-Corpse?"

"Darn it, Hank. Where have you been for the last hour?"

"I—I—"

"Forget it," Remington said. "I'll do it myself." And then he walked us down the hall. He sat me down on a plastic chair outside a room with a thick wooden door. "You wait here. Hey, Hank. Hank, you listening?"

Hank poked his shaved head around the corner, eyes wide. "Yeah?"

"Keep an eye on her, will ya?"

And then he escorted Hentie and Barkington into the interview room. The door clicked shut.

Hank stood down the hallway, shifting his weight from one foot to the other and watching me as if I was about to leap up and start throwing hands. "You want anything to drink? A water or anything like that?"

"That would be great, thanks."

Hank hurried off, clearly glad to be out of my presence. I sat back with my arms folded, and shut my eyes. I focused on my breathing, allowing the awareness of the long hallway to wash over me. The cream lacquered walls, the old wooden floor that was polished from years of use, and the smell of paperwork and coffee, stale cigarette smoke.

Cigarette smoke. Cigarette butt.

But who did it belong to?

Given the victim's strong feelings about drinking, I doubted that she was a smoker. And the choice of murder weapon was so obvious. The ethanol was a callback to her hatred of a "fun time" as Hadley had put it.

Which definitely shifted the young redhead to the top of my list. She had mentioned Victoria's penchant for being a stick in the mud repeatedly. But Hadley had also been with us on the night that the murder had allegedly taken place. And how on earth would either woman have known about the secret room?

There were other issues at play.

The stolen heirloom. The dark figure creeping around the outside of the Dawson residence, hiding between the trees. The sister.

A phone rang in the other room.

The sister.

There was a thought. The ever-silent sister. Where had she been on that night? What if the murder hadn't taken place that night?

Victoria's clothes say otherwise.

Could have taken place in the early hours of the morning, but I would surely have heard something. And Bark would have too. And Smulder.

So how?

Footsteps creaked in the adjacent room, and I opened my eyes as good ol' Deputy Hank rounded the corner with a polystyrene cup of water.

"Thanks," I said, accepting it from him with a bob of my head. "Long day?"

"No, but if what the sheriff said was true, it's about to be."

He hovered in the hallway again, folding and unfolding his arms.

"I'm not going to make a run for it, if that's what you're worried about," I said. "I've got nowhere else to be."

Hank retreated into the open plan office area, the squeak of an office chair indicating he'd taken his seat. I set the cup of water aside without taking a sip and wiped my hands on my shirt. I'd been a spy long enough to know you didn't drink from an open glass of water.

I closed my eyes again.

The sister was an interesting potential suspect. But what would her motive be? And why had Dale Dunnels wanted to talk to Victoria? Another avenue to investigate.

Again, footsteps sounded in the room adjacent. This time, the clip of heels. Deputy Hank's chair squeaked and there was a heavy thump as something hit the floor. "M-Mayor Barrera! What are you doing here?"

"You ought to be careful how you sit, Hank," the mayor replied. "You could break a tailbone falling out of an office chair at that height."

Deputy Hank gave a timid giggle.

"I need to see the sheriff. Where is he?"

"He's in the middle of an interrogation, Mayor, ma'am, sir," Hank said, then coughed. "I mean Mayor Barrera."

"Easy, Hank. I'm not an auditor or your boss." Her tone was relaxed, but there was an edge to it. Not the same anxious edge she'd had when she'd led the town hall meeting. This was deeper. A tension that had seeped into every word. I didn't blame her.

Victoria, dead, and in such a strange manner. This would look bad for the town, especially one that relied more and more on tourism thanks to the lake.

"I need to see the sheriff, right away," Mayor Barrera said.

"But I— He told me—"

"Trust me, Hank. This is important."

The deputy's hurried footsteps came around the corner. I didn't open my eyes.

A knock rattled the wooden door, and there was a muttered curse from within. "What do you want, Hank?" Sheriff Remington snapped.

"Mayor Barrera is here to see you, Sheriff. She said it's important."

"Of course, it's important, Hank. She's the darn mayor." The door clicked, and the sheriff passed me by the scent of deodorant, sweat, and cigarette smoke following him.

"Mayor," Sheriff Remington said. "You heard?"

"I heard."

"I would invite you into my office to talk," the sheriff said, "but I'm in the middle of interviewing one of the suspects."

"I understand," the Mayor said, then hesitated.

Silence.

"Hank," Sheriff Remington said. "Scram, will ya? Go outside and catch some sunlight. Take a smoke break."

"But I don't smoke."

"Do something before I fire you."

"Yes, Sheriff, sir." Hank left the room but didn't enter the hallway. I kept my eyes shut, tuning into my senses. These two had no idea who I was. They wouldn't care that I was in the hall, mostly because the mayor was unaware and the sheriff was proving increasingly inept.

"This is bad news, Colton," the mayor said, her tone dropping low. "With the Thanksgiving parade coming up? And the way folks have been so keyed up about stranger danger and tourism?"

"Only one who complained was Victoria," Remington said.

"Yeah, and look how that turned out," the mayor whispered. "I need you to keep this as quiet as possible."

"Quiet!" The sheriff yelled the word. "Now, Mayor, how in the heck do you expect me to do that? We haven't had a murder in Tickle in... not since I've been in charge, unless you're counting the time Abby Zanders dove into the shallow end of the pool and—"

"Keep your voice down," Barrera said. "There's no need to panic. We'll handle this. But we have to be careful about it. We'll call it a suspicious death, not a homicide, all right?"

"I can't do that. If she was murdered, I got to do my due diligence." At least he had some measure of a spine.

"Don't be a fool, Colton. I'm not saying that you don't investigate. I'm saying that you keep it quiet. As quiet as you can until you've figured out what happened. The best case scenario is that we find out this was a terrible mistake. If you catch my meaning."

Another breadth of silence.

"You're saying I just, uh, keep it quiet."

"I'm saying that this will all turn out to be one big accident, and if it is an accident, we really don't want it splashed all over the news that we thought it was something bigger than what it was. It's Thanksgiving, Colton, people want to spend time with their families, not worry about grizzly murders."

"But the newspaper, the local news—"

"You let me worry about them. You just keep this close to your chest." A patting sound. "There's a good man." Barrera's heels clicked away.

The sheriff didn't say a word or move for a good minute. Finally, he rounded the corner and headed back into his office. Either, he didn't notice me or he didn't care.

But I appreciated the oversight. They'd just given me another clue to add to the growing list.

Eight

HENTIE AND I ARRIVED BACK AT THE HOUSE TO find that the cops had sealed the room where the body had been with a sticker. Otherwise, we were granted entry into the house and the ability to live there, even though the investigation wasn't complete. Given what I'd heard, I wasn't surprised.

"I think I'm going to lie down," Hentie said. "It's been a long day."

It was late, and Hentie had waited for Sheriff Remington to finish questioning me before we'd come home. The ride back had been fraught with tension, while my mind ran circles around the images and suspicions on my corkboard.

"You don't want anything to eat first?" I asked.

"No. I'll just have a nap. Maybe I'll have a midnight

snack or something, but I just want to go to bed, April. I can't believe they found that woman's body in my house. And right after Franklin died."

I couldn't quite believe it either, and that was saying a lot. I'd seen my fair share of nonsensical things.

Hentie and Barkington headed upstairs. I double-checked the front door was locked, as well as all the down-stairs windows, then went up to the second floor as well. I didn't blame Hentie for wanting to go straight to bed.

I stifled a yawn as I headed for my bedroom, passing paneled walls and paintings that made me wonder. How many other secret rooms were there in this mansion?

If this place was old, old enough to have been built during prohibition times, then the hidden rooms might hearken back to that time. Who had owned this house before Franklin had bought it? Fascinating.

I opened my bedroom door, expecting darkness, and found the lights on, my closet door open, and a half-packed suitcase on my bed.

"What the—?"

Smulder emerged from the closet, holding an armful of my clothes.

"Have you lost what's left of your ever-loving mind?" I asked, shutting the door behind me. "What are you doing?"

"I'm getting you out of here."

"Huh?"

"We're leaving tonight. Now."

"I take it you found out about the corpse in the hidden room," I said, and folded my arms. "Oliver, you can't be serious."

"I have never," he said, dumping the clothes into the bag, "been more serious"—another armful tossed in—"about anything in my life."

"Brian," I hissed, using his real name rather than his code name. "I'm not abandoning Hentie and Barkington."

"Oh, but you are. You don't have a choice. If you stay here we're all going to die."

"You're blowing this out of proportion."

"No," Smulder said, advancing on me. "You're not taking this seriously enough. Grandpa told you that there are unsavory people looking for you and your family, and this happens *in the house*?"

"You think it's a threat? A message?"

"It could be. Who's to say?"

"They'd kill you or me if they had the power to do that. We live in the same house," I said. "You're not thinking clearly."

"How do you expect me to think clearly, when it's so obvious that you are in mortal danger and you won't take me seriously!"

The words rang through the room.

I swallowed.

Brian took great, deep breaths and turned his head so that he didn't have to look at me. Or so that I wouldn't see how emotional this had made him.

"This is not the first time you've done this," I said. "You're getting ahead of yourself. A murder has been committed, but trust me, it's not going to make headline news."

Brian frowned. "What makes you say that?"

I told him about the mayor's conversation with the sheriff.

"More reason to leave," Brian said. "The law enforcement officials here aren't to be trusted. They might see you as an easy target and decide to make you the fall guy. You'll be dead the minute your face hits the papers, April. It won't be long until they find you."

"You need to stop." I put up a palm. "I understand your distress and your concern, but I'm not leaving Hentie and Bark."

"And what about me?" he asked quietly. "If I left, what then?"

I choked on thin air. "What?"

"You're focused on saving your friend and her dog. But what about me? Aren't we friends, April?"

"Don't manipulate me," I said. "They can't look after themselves as well as we can. You'd be fine on your own."

"I see," Brian said. "I see. All right. That settles it then." He slapped the suitcase shut and walked to my bedroom door. "You stay, Delta. You stay here and you put yourself and your friends and your entire family in danger because you won't listen to sense. See how well that plays out for you. You've made my job impossible."

And then he left the room and slammed the door shut behind him so hard, the window panes rattled.

I released a breath.

Darn. That had not gone well.

You should have kept your cool. But it was difficult when faced with him panicking. I'd never met someone like Brian before, but he was also... It was complicated with him. And he didn't understand that we couldn't just run every time something happened.

Often, the best option was patience. A cool head.

Snap decisions could lead to disaster.

I walked through my bedroom at Hentie's house—a guestroom with white walls, a picture of a field of sunflowers opposite the comfy bed—and plopped down on the cream sheets. I hadn't yet drawn my curtains on the view of the outside world.

This room was so close to where the murder had taken place.

How had I not heard anything? It was an indictment on my spy skills that this had gone unnoticed.

The tension wouldn't ease out of my limbs. I couldn't focus on anything but the murder, and Smulder's pained expression as he stood in front of me, declaring how reckless I was for not leaving town.

I clicked off my bedside lamp and stared at the cream satin lampshade in the dark. I'd figure this out. I had to.

My phone buzzed in my pocket.

Huh.

Grant? At nine o' clock at night? Maybe, if he'd heard about the murder. Had Smulder told him?

But the number on the screen wasn't saved.

I answered it. "Hello?"

"April Waters." The voice was impossibly deep—the caller was using a voice changer.

My eyes narrowed, my vision tunneling as I flicked through the possibilities in a millisecond. Had to be an enemy who'd gotten hold of my number, which meant I had to get rid of this phone immediately. And that Brian was right. We had to leave.

"Wrong number," I said.

"Don't hang up, April," the voice said. "I'm a friend."

"A friend." The word came out sardonically. I highly doubted that.

"A friend," they repeated. "You're in danger."

"You don't say," I replied. "Me? Under imminent threat of death? Gee, I'm shocked."

The person on the end cleared their throat. "I mean, you don't have to be sarcastic." The way they phrased it was familiar and also comical, given the voice changer. "I'm trying to help you catch a break. You've always been—"

"Been what? Who is this?"

"If you want to find out and save your friends and family, come to the old observatory across the Tickle Lake at midnight tonight."

"How did you get this number?"

They didn't answer.

"Hello? How did you—"

"I've got friends in low places." And then the line went dead.

I pulled the phone from my ear and stared at it. I brought my nerves under control, practicing my breathing, and squeezed the phone in my palm.

A mystical warning from a stranger who had my number? I had my suspicions.

I got off the bed, grabbed my fanny pack of spy tools, and then let myself out into the house. *I hope I'm not making a terrible mistake.*

Nine

I MOVED, SHADOWLIKE, THROUGH THE underbrush, taking a circuitous route toward the Tickleton Observatory. I'd brought my mind to a focused point, remaining in the present and concentrating on the sounds of the night.

Any snap of a twig or rustle caught my attention.

This was a foolish thing to do, but my gut had told me that coming out here was a good idea rather than a bad one.

The closer I drew toward the observatory, the more focused I became.

My steps were whisper quiet, as I moved around the trunks of trees in the dark, heading toward the chain link fence. Tonight, the moon was a waning crescent, just past its full moon peak, and it cast plenty of light along the water—a midnight surface, smooth and without ripple.

I stopped beside the chain link fence, scanning the surroundings.

A prickle ran down my spine.

A noise, infinitesimal in comparison to the night ambience, behind me. Light enough to be ignored by anyone else.

I spun around, bringing my hand out and aiming for the side of the neck.

But my attacker caught my wrist and stopped me before I could hit my mark.

"Really, Delta," a woman said, her British accent distinct, "the vagus nerve? You ought to try something new once in a while."

I dropped my hand and held back a whoop of excitement. "Gamma?"

My grandmother, an ex-spy, who was the most decorated veteran in the NSIB, gave me a joyful smile in response. She wore an all-black suit of body armor and a black beanie pulled over her neatly cut gray hair.

I threw my arms around her and hugged her tight, a wedge of emotion rising in my throat. "What are you doing here?"

Gamma patted my back awkwardly—she'd never been great with physical displays of affection. "We came to give you some much needed insight. And tell you our plans."

"We?"

Charlotte, my cousin, stepped out from behind a tree, her hair dyed a shade of red that was similar to the color I'd had when I'd been undercover in Gossip, Texas, visiting them.

"What's going on?" I asked.

"And hello to you too, Delta." Charlie came forward.

I hugged her. "Sorry. I'm a little tense."

"Yeah, we heard about it," Charlie said, and drew back, studying me with a concerned gaze. We'd had our moments, but she was my cousin, and when things went in the wrong direction, she'd always be there for me. My family was something I could always count on.

"What are you doing here?" I asked.

"Usually, I'd prefer to conduct my business in a comfortable underground bunker," Gamma said. "But given the current set of circumstances, it seems that will *not* be possible."

"Grant called us," Charlie said. "He told us about a leak at the NSIB, and the possibility that there are shady characters around looking for you, and for us."

"A leak?" I flushed red hot. "He didn't tell me about a leak."

"Typical," Charlie said. "He's a real pain in the rear-end, isn't he?" Charlie leaned casually against a tree, her arms folded. She was blunt whenever the occasion called for it. And, in her opinion, it called for it most of the time. "I don't envy you whatever you're about to go through."

"Charlotte, come now. We don't need to upset her any more than she already is."

"So, you came all the way out here to tell me about the leak?" Obviously, that wasn't the case. But they hadn't given me their reasoning yet. "What's going on?"

"Grant told us we've got to get out of Gossip for a while," Charlie said, her tone an irritable growl. "You know, just leave behind everything we've built, our homes, families, the people we love—"

"Charlotte," Gamma said, raising a gloved palm. "We discussed this."

"I'm supposed to be happy about this? They put Lauren in a protection program. She's pregnant, Georgina."

"Everything they've done has been for a good reason. Complaining about our current lot in life is not going to help. This too shall pass."

"That's very Gandalf of you," Charlie grumbled.

"No."

Both of them turned to look at me.

"Sorry, it's just that Gandalf said 'you shall not pass.'"

Nobody misquoted Tolkien on my watch, especially not in the heat of danger. "So, you're going on the run?"

"Temporarily." Gamma waved a hand so that Charlie wouldn't interject. "And we'll be back as soon as we can. I don't necessarily like leaving the inn for any period of time, but we've come up with an elegant solution."

"Which is?"

Charlie sniffed. "Gamma has signed off the Gossip Inn to Jessie Belle-Blue, temporarily. Madness. Absolute madness."

"On occasion, it's necessary to put one's ego in one's pocket," Gamma said.

The quiet trees, the moon, glinting off the glass dome of the observatory made the night peaceful. This conversation was anything but. "I appreciate you letting me know that you're leaving."

"We didn't come out here to tell you that we're leaving," Charlie said, clicking her knuckles. She wore a similar bodysuit to my grandmother's. Gamma had had them specially made, and she'd made one for me too, though I'd left it behind when my cover in Gossip had been blown.

The pain of that time came swimming back. The image of my ex's body rose to the surface, and I had to force it back down.

"You're coming with us," Charlie said.

"I—what now? You've got to be out of your mind."

"I beg your very best pardon?" Gamma pressed a hand to her chest.

"Sorry, Gamma, not you specifically."

"Then who?" Charlie arched both dark eyebrows at me.

I sighed. "I'm not leaving Tickle."

"Why not?" Charlie asked. "We're telling you that danger's inbound, and you're unwilling to leave? That doesn't seem like the incredibly logical and robotic Delta I know and... begrudgingly like."

"Thanks." It came out flat. I'd worked on my social skills repeatedly. I wasn't too blunt or too soft, and I hid the fact that I had a photographic memory and a penchant for organizing everything to a tee from those around me. It stung that Charlie found me "robotic."

"What's going on, dear?" Gamma asked.

She hardly ever used terms of endearment. "I have people to look after," I said. "I'm not the only one who's at risk."

"Yeah, we have no idea how that feels," Charlie said. "Did you miss the part about Lauren? The town?"

"I heard you," I said, wishing for once that my cousin wasn't so darn to the point. "I heard you. But the people I have to look after don't know anything about who I am. Not really. And if I leave, it will put a target on their backs." Bark and Hentie were already at risk because of their proximity to me. I should have listened to Smulder at the start and avoided having them join us.

Charlie threw up her hands. "So much for our family vacation."

"Charlotte, give us a moment." Gamma took me by the elbow, gently, and guided me closer toward the lake, the image of the moon reflected in its calm waters. She halted and gave me that sharp blue-eyed gaze that cut straight to the heart of a matter.

"Are you sure about this?" Gamma asked. "Are you entirely certain that you want to stay? There would be no better way to hide than with us."

The temptation was there. To run off with Gamma and Charlie, spend time traveling the country or even leaving entirely, would be a slice of heaven. I'd be able to relax with them, to a certain extent, not only because Georgina Mission, my capable Gamma, would be in charge, but because I'd be free. Free of the pressures of what was going on with Smulder. And free of worrying about Hentie and Bark.

Except that wasn't true, was it? I'd always be worried about them or sure that someone was out to get them. Because I'd put them at risk. If the people who were after me couldn't find me, they'd use Hentie and Bark as collateral.

I glanced back at Charlie, who watched us through narrowed eyes.

"I'm sure," I said. "I can't run away and leave others to clean up this mess. This is my fault."

Gamma placed a hand on my cheek and patted it gently. "Don't be too hard on yourself, Delta. We all make mistakes, and you've made less of them than the rest of us. We'll be in touch."

"With or without the voice changer?" I whispered.

Gamma laughed. "I think you know." She gave me a hug goodbye. Charlie waved at me from the tree, and the pair headed off into the darkness together, leaving me with my thoughts and my regrets.

And the sound of... humming?

Where was that coming from?

Ten

The humming was faint.

I turned in a circle looking for the source. The observatory was silent, the dome eerie in the darkness, unlit and abandoned. Was there someone inside or—

The humming grew a little louder then stopped, and it was in the quiet that I faced the lake and spotted a dark figure standing on the opposite shore. I didn't move, feeling out whether they'd noticed me yet.

Who are you?

Was it the person who had robbed the Dawson home of the heirloom Victoria had mentioned?

Whoever they were, they were clearly enjoying the evening, and they weren't worried about being seen or heard. The figure bent and picked at the grass or something hidden in it, then skipped off between the trees toward the Dawson house.

They hadn't seen me.

I narrowed my eyes, watching their progress toward the double story home, with its eerie aesthetic—a steepled roof, the windows darkened, and the porch lights off. Like a crooked witch's house from a horror movie.

The person moved onto the path in front of the house, and into the slanting beams of moonlight, revealing dark hair draped across her back and a pale complexion. She held a cigarette in her hand and puffed on it.

Emery Dawson.

It had to be her. The quiet sister who had sat beside Victoria in the town hall, her head bent and her eyes downward cast.

What on earth was she doing out in the middle of the night, skipping along the river bank and humming a tune to herself? *And smoking.* Not the picture of the grieving sister. In comparison to how she'd behaved at that town hall meeting, she was downright joyful.

I took a snapshot of her on that pathway and added it to the corkboard in my mind. My heart skipped at the sight of another image on the board, one I hadn't placed there when Victoria's body had been found.

This image was fuzzy, out of focus and, frustratingly, I

was sure that it was the answer to what had happened to the victim. A way to save Hentie from undue scrutiny and to keep Smulder and Special Agent in Charge Grant off my back.

Emery stubbed her cigarette and disappeared into the Dawson house, and the lights turned on inside. First the foyer, visible through a misted glass window, and then, minutes later, the tiny attic window lit up—a yellow circle against the black backdrop of the building.

Huh. What are you up to Emery?

I walked back to a nearby tree and sat beneath it, between two gnarled roots, my tree pressed against rough bark.

The truth was, I'd made my decision. I wouldn't be leaving Hentie and Bark behind. Special Agent in Charge Grant didn't need an update because the mayor was making sure that this death stayed under wraps—exceedingly suspicious. I had time. Time to figure out what had happened and keep Hentie's name clear and out of the papers, along with my own. Time to hide in plain sight and run when whoever was looking for me arrived in town.

Irresponsible. Dangerous!

I unzipped my fanny pack—or my spy utility belt as Smulder preferred to call it—and went through the items within, neatly categorized and tucked into side pouches and special loops. I removed a silver cylinder, about the size of my middle finger, as well as a tiny chrome pill. I tapped the pill and opened it, revealing the miniature drone within.

The FlyBoy Drone was part of the repertoire of high-tech spy tools I'd been given to use during my time on the run. I twisted the cylinder on either end and the drone activated and buzzed into the night sky in front of my face, hovering there.

I rotated the cylinder—a remote that unlocked and unfolded to project a holographic image of what the drone saw as it flew—then directed the drone across the water.

The drone zipped over the lake, and I weaved it past the trees. First, I swept it down toward the grass where Emery stood humming. She'd left a single flower—a black rose—underneath an old oak.

Could it be that the humming was part of her farewell to her sister? But why leave a rose under this particular tree? Did it have special significance to the family? To Victoria?

I took a mental image of it then swept the drone toward the house.

The cigarette butt wasn't the same make of cigarette as the butt at the crime scene. This one's filter was white and long, whereas the cigarette butt at the scene had been yellow and stubby. That didn't rule Emery out.

I directed my buddy toward the porch.

I didn't bother looking for cracks to get inside and investigate. My goal was to spy on Emery through that top window. When in doubt, take the easiest route.

The drone zipped upward, and I hovered it in front of the attic window, the panes of glass clean enough to make out what was going on inside.

"What the—?" I murmured, under my breath, adjusting the FlyBoy mid-air to get a better look.

Emery flitted from table to table inside, lighting column candles. Once she was done, she walked toward the attic door and grabbed an apron from a peg attached to it. She tied on the apron then clicked off the attic fluorescents, so that the flicker from the candles lit the room. And then she minced toward a covered stand on the opposite end of the vast space.

I didn't have sound on the remote, but I could almost hear the creak of those old wooden floorboards as she moved across them.

Emery lifted her hands to the sky, spun in a circle, and then grabbed the end of the fabric cover and ripped it down to reveal...

A painting.

That's anticlimactic.

Or was it?

Emery made quick work of arranging brushes, paints, and a cup of water to the left of the artwork.

Weird or not, the painting was breathtaking.

Gentle brushstrokes and colors had brought the item in the center of the painting to life.

A huge brass key, old with a patina from years of use, lying on a blue velvet cushion. Emery had done such a fantastic job of painting it, it looked as if I could reach out and pluck the key off the painting and walk away with it. Assuming I could carry a key that was half the size of my body.

Seriously, the artwork was huge.

But why a key?

I took a snapshot of the image, both with my FlyBoy drone and my mind, before Emery stood in front of it again, cupping a hand under her pointed chin and examining her work.

A key.

A key to what?

A locked room. Hentie's secret room?

I'd gotten into that room with the press of a button. There hadn't been a lock.

Potentially, I was reading too much into this. Emery

might enjoy painting, and the key might be practice. But my gut said there was more to it than that.

I tapped the FlyBoy Drone down on the window sill to preserve its battery, directing it toward the key and examining the painting in more detail.

The top of the key was composed of three brass interlocking circles, leading down toward the long shaft of the key itself. Ornate teeth glowed golden in the flickering candlelight, decorated in floral patterns.

Emery set to work on the painting again, adding more definition with touches of paint here or there. I was about as artistic as an ice cream cone—her process was magic to me.

I took another mental image of the painting for good measure, then directed the FlyBoy Drone back across the lake. I opened my palm and landed it in my hand before powering down the remote and tucking the little buddy back into his chrome housing.

Everything went back into my fanny pack, tucked neatly into place.

Tonight had given me plenty to think about. My family was taking a prolonged vacation from Texas because of me, Smulder was furious, and Hentie needed help.

If I left, I endangered Hentie. If I stayed, I endangered myself.

Either way, I'd avoid trouble by figuring out who'd

killed Victoria and tucked her away in Hentie's castle-like home. And why.

I got up, sparing a final glance for the strange house across the lake, the creepy light from the attic window a reminder of what I'd witnessed.

Emery Dawson had officially made the list.

Eleven

HENTIE AND I TOOK BREAKFAST IN THE expansive kitchen in her mansion-like home at nine in the morning. I made the coffee, while my friend prepared the eggs and bacon. Bark watched us from the rough wooden table near the back door, his head peeking at us over the table edge.

The kitchen was the warmest, friendliest part of the house with cream tiles, copper pots hanging over a center island and a view of the back yard with the woods fringing the low fence. While Hentie's home was impressive, beautiful even, it was also kind of creepy. The hidden rooms, the creaking stairs, the occasional bump in the night. The atmosphere was amplified by the discovery of Victoria Dawson's corpse.

And those lipstick 'x' marks on her cheeks.

X marks the spot? Or was this related to something else?

And lipstick. Lipstick could be bought or used by anyone. This didn't mean the killer was a woman.

I poured coffee into mugs while I pondered, glancing out of the archway and into the living room. A grandfather clock ticked nearby.

Smulder hadn't come down this morning. I doubted he was sleeping in. I was certain he didn't want to talk to me this morning, and that was fine. I had Hentie and Bark and an unsolved murder case to deal with.

I sat at the table on my phone, fiddling with a new app I'd been developing for my spy work. Hentie wouldn't be able to see it from where she was positioned, but I kept an eye on her regardless.

The app was meant to hack into people's phones, but it was buggy and irritating the heck out of me this morning. It was a good distraction from yesterday's events.

Hentie yawned, pressing the back of her hand to her mouth. "Jinne, but I'm tired this morning."

"Understandable," I said, locking my phone and setting it aside. "What with the dead body in the hidden room. And of course, your husband."

She gave me a smile. "I'm so happy you brought the truck to Tickle," she said. "Especially since you have those special circumstances you never want to tell me about."

Hentie knew that I couldn't reveal my true identity, but she wasn't sure why. And I'd keep it that way.

Bark gave a yip to include himself in the conversation.

"I wouldn't dream of being anywhere else," I said. "Traveling on the truck with you and Bark has been a highlight for me."

Hentie grinned and turned the bacon over in the pan, the spit and crack and delicious salty smell made my stomach growl.

"I had a call from Franklin's solicitor today. The executor of the will," Hentie said, brushing her hands off on her frilly pink apron. "He wants to talk to me next week after Thanksgiving."

"I can't believe you hadn't heard from him until now."

"The funeral policy covered the expenses for Franklin's affairs," Hentie replied, and then bowed her head, shutting her eyes. "I've been putting it off, jong. I didn't want to face the fact that he's gone. But it's time."

I went over and gave her a hug. "I'm sorry."

"Thank you." She patted my back. "Will you be present when he's here, asseblief? I need moral support."

"I'll be here." I gave her a reassuring squeeze of the arm, then returned to my cup of coffee. I set out two plates for breakfast, but a copy of the local newspaper on the kitchen counter caught my eye.

Terrible Accident Claims Upstanding Citizen in Tickle, Texas. Sheriff Lacks Answers.

Tickle, TX. Sheriff Remington of the Howard County Sheriff's Department called a conference late last night to discuss the untimely passing of Miss Victoria Dawson. Miss Dawson was an upstanding citizen who attended every town hall meeting, and was the head of the Tickle Ethics Committee. A treasured member of Tickle, she will be sorely missed, especially by her only living family member, her sister, Emery Dawson.

The shocking death, mere days before The Tickle Thanksgiving Parade and festivities, has drawn attention, speculation and incited fear among local residents, but Remington, the long-standing sheriff, believes there's nothing to be concerned about.

"This is most likely a case of accidental poisoning," the sheriff said, at the untelevised conference last night. "Unfortunately, Miss Dawson was drinking irresponsibly. But we're keeping the case open and investigating to our fullest capacity, because we know that the citizens of Tickle want answers."

When asked why he would need to investigate when the poisoning was accidental, the sheriff claimed that while the death was likely accidental, they had to ensure that there was no foul play.

"For now, folks can rest assured that the Thanksgiving

Parade will proceed as usual, and that the holiday weekend will go uninterrupted. There's nothing to worry about. No killer on the loose or anything like that."

With Thanksgiving coming up tomorrow, residents of Tickle should be grateful to spend the day with loved ones. Miss Emery Dawson, the sister of the deceased, won't be so lucky.

That was an ominous last line.

Emery Dawson alone on Thanksgiving day? An idea occurred to me.

"Say, Hentie?"

"Ja."

"What do you think about inviting some people over for Thanksgiving?"

"Who did you have in mind?" Hentie asked, as she dished bacon onto a kitchen towel.

"Emery Dawson," I said, and tapped the newspaper.

Hentie's gray bun bobbled as she walked over. She read the newspaper, lifting it in both hands and bringing it close to her face. "I need reading glasses," she said. "You think she was the one who killed Victoria?"

"I don't know," I said. "But she's going to be alone on Thanksgiving. And we won't have much else to do after the parade except eat and chat."

"They're not going to investigate it properly," Hentie

said, her lips pursed as she flicked the newspaper aside. "Remington is so…"

"Annoying?"

"Ongelooflik," she said. "Unbelievable. He asked me the dumbest questions when he interviewed me the other day. And he didn't seem like he wanted to figure out what was going on."

"Was that before or after he left the room?"

Hentie delivered the plates to the kitchen table, then broke off a piece of her bacon and gave it to Barkington to nibble on. "After. Why?"

"Because I overheard him talking to the mayor." And then I gave Hentie the down low. The mayor didn't want Thanksgiving interrupted or law enforcement, potentially the FBI or the CID—the Criminal Investigations Division—descending on the town. She wanted everything to go smoothly. "But is there more to it than that?" I pondered out loud.

"I didn't know any of these people well," Hentie said. "Like I've mentioned before, I was often away from home and so was Franklin. But Victoria had a reputation for being full of it."

"The mayor didn't like her either," I said. "I could tell by the way she talked to her when she was leading the town meeting. She didn't want her interfering. And Victoria made a scene about it."

Hentie sat down as I placed the coffee mugs on the breakfast table. I took my place across from her.

"But how did they get into my house?" Hentie asked.

"The front gates were open for the party, right? Anyone could have slipped in and out at any time," I said.

"But Victoria left. And I *always* lock my doors."

That was the puzzle. I ate a slice of bacon and mulled it over, considering my corkboard and the fuzzy picture attached to it. A red thread connected it to the image of Victoria's body. A cigarette butt. The alcohol that had been injected directly into her system. The 'x' marks on her cheeks.

Accidental my booty.

"The mayor has to be included as a suspect," I said, pushing my eggs around my plate. "As well as Hadley, since she hated Victoria and kept accusing her of ruining everyone's fun."

"And the sister too," Hentie said, her shoulders drawing backward. She wore black today, as she'd done for weeks now, but it had been a while since I'd seen excitement in her bright green eyes. She needed a distraction from the stress and sorrow.

And man, there was nothing like taking control of your destiny. Even if it landed you in trouble.

"We've got a full day ahead of us," I said. "Should we serve ice cream? Go pay the mayor a visit?"

"We could. She's got an open door policy. She gives out her number to anyone who will take it," Hentie said. "But she's always busy."

"Huh." I couldn't quit thinking about the painting I'd seen in Emery's attic, or the fact that Hadley had hated Victoria. And what about the theft at the Dawson family home? Or the way the mayor wanted to keep things under wraps?

All roads led back to the Dawson house.

"Let's serve up some ice cream," I said. "And when we're done, I've got our first lead."

Hentie wriggled in her seat and fed Barkington, who had taken up a spot in her lap, another piece of bacon. I hadn't seen her this excited in a long time, and it helped assure me that I'd made the right decision last night. To stay and help.

Twelve

"At least Remington won't come looking for us," Hentie said. "Since he doesn't care about whether this was a murder or not."

We had finished up on the ice cream truck after a long afternoon serving customers who varied between suspicious to chatty. Tickle locals, or the Ticklers, as they liked to call themselves, were obsessed with what had happened to Victoria.

The theories were wild, but none of them were as crazy as the truth. That she'd been found in a locked, secret room. And that there was no possible way for her to have gotten in there.

But that's not true, is it?

Where there was a will, there was a way.

It was a pleasant afternoon, a stark contrast to the

weather I'd encountered in the North, and I enjoyed every minute of it. I wasn't built for the cold. I dished up several scoops of Neapolitan ice cream into a cup then handed it to Hentie.

She grabbed a wooden paddle from the holder on the food truck's counter then headed toward the back to grab Bark from his crate. I dished up a cup of ice cream for myself and joined her at a bench overlooking the lake. It was beautiful, the observatory's glass dome barely visible between the trees, and the lake sunlit.

The dark specter of the Dawson house loomed across the water.

"What do you think?" Hentie asked. "Will the sheriff bother us?"

"No," I said. "I doubt it. He's preoccupied with the Thanksgiving parade tomorrow, and the mayor will be too. Now's the perfect time for us to do a little unorthodox snooping." I checked my watch. Just past three. "I say we finish our ice cream then drive out there." I gestured toward the Dawson house with my ice cream paddle. "Emery's got to have some answers."

Barkington barked and turned in a circle in Hentie's lap, desperate for a lick of ice cream. "Te veel suiker, Blaffies." She paused. "Too much sugar," she added for my benefit.

"We should make dog ice cream," I said.

Hentie made a gagging noise. "Is jy mal? Are you mad?"

"Huh?"

"An ice cream made out of dogs? I thought I knew you, April. That is the most vile—"

"Whoa," I said, holding up a palm, my ice cream paddle clasped between my thumb and forefinger. "I meant ice cream that's safe for dogs to eat."

"Oh. Oh." She laughed and pressed her hand to her forehead. "Sorry. I've been assuming the worst lately, after the body and... everything." She'd chosen another black pantsuit today.

I squeezed her arm. "We'll distract ourselves with the case."

"That's a good idea."

We finished our treat and deposited the empty cups in a nearby recycling receptacle. The expenses for the food truck were paid for by the NSIB. Thankfully, I could ask for whatever I needed from Grant when it came to the truck. The same wasn't true for my freedom of movement.

Hentie strapped her caramel-colored pup back into his crate, and we took the drive around the lake, on a dirt road that circled it and led past storied houses.

"This town is so rich in history," I said.

An image flashed into my mind. The 'x' marks on Victoria's cheeks in bright red lipstick.

I slowed the truck as we approached the Dawson house. "What do you know about Emery?"

"Not much," Hentie said, adjusting her seatbelt and craning her neck at the house looming between the trees.

There was that circular attic window. Unlit today.

I directed the truck down the long road that led toward the building—it was creepier on this side—and parked near the steps that led up to a wooden wraparound porch. A Honda was parked nearby.

Our plan was to ply Emery with ice cream, or offer our condolences.

Hentie grabbed Barkington, and we took the porch steps together. The house itself had a weighty atmosphere, both dark and mysterious. I raised my fist to knock, and the forest went still, as if there was a predator nearby, waiting to attack.

Barkington whined in Hentie's arms. "I don't like this," Hentie whispered. "Why's it so quiet?"

I broke the silence with my knock, unintimidated. But I scanned the treeline on either side of the house, searching for ominous figures or watching enemies. With the news that I was in danger, I couldn't let my guard down. I shifted so that I could block Hentie and Bark from harm, should an enemy appear and try to take a shot.

Emery didn't come to the door. Was she even home?

What did we know about the sister of the deceased?

She was quiet, she liked to paint, and she'd hummed that tune under the tree late last night. It had almost seemed ritualistic.

Ritual markings on the cheeks? Don't know about that.

"Let's go around the back. Maybe she's out by the lake," I said.

Hentie, Bark and I headed back down the steps and around the side of the house. I was keenly aware of the potential for an ambush, and I feigned calm in my posture, breathing evenly while my gaze roved over the trees. Nothing. No one.

Two figures near the lake, under the tree where I'd found the black rose with the FlyBoy Drone.

My hand closed around Hentie's arm, and I pulled her toward the side of the house, hiding us from view.

Barkington whined.

"Quiet, please, Bark," I murmured. "There are people over there."

"Jinne, April," Hentie breathed, "I didn't even see them yet. You're very quick."

I had to be. "Stay here." I pressed my back to the side of the house and slinked along it until I reached the corner. I relaxed my shoulders and checked the treeline, exposing as little of my head as possible.

Emery stood beneath the tree where she'd left the flower, her hands clasped together as she faced a man in a lime green suit with hair that stood out at odd angles. Dale Dunnels, the man we'd seen twice now—at the memorial for Hentie's husband and at the carnival grounds. He'd been looking for Victoria that morning.

What was he doing talking to Emery?

Perhaps, talking wasn't the right word. He was questioning her, but she didn't open her mouth to answer. She backed against the tree, putting her hands out and shaking her head without making a sound.

"—tell the truth! If you don't, you'll get in trouble for it." His words drifted over.

I didn't like his tone or the way he was advancing on her, but it wasn't time to interfere yet. I took a mental image of them for my corkboard, and a thin red line traveled from the picture to another of Emery and Victoria at the townhall. A second string connected it to Dunnels at the carnival grounds, asking for Victoria.

"You can't pretend any longer. I know you can talk!"

Emery couldn't talk? But I'd heard her humming the other day? If she couldn't talk, then it wasn't because of damage to her vocal chords. Another reason then? Psychological or physiological? Or a choice?

"This is ridiculous. I came for answers, and I want them, do you hear?"

Emery shook her head, frantically.

Dale sighed and backed up. "Useless. What was I thinking? Coming here to talk to an invalid."

Huh. This guy was a scumbag.

He turned on his booted heel and charged in my direction. I pressed myself back and waited. Hentie and Bark looked on nearby, their eyes comically wide.

Mr. Dunnels turned the corner, and I stuck out a leg. He yelped, his arms flailing as he tipped forward. I let him fall before grabbing the back of his lurid lime suit jacket and jerking him upright. "Careful, Mr. Dunnels," I said, quietly, to the portly man. "Wouldn't want to take a spill and break something."

Dunnels gasped and struggled. I released him and gave a bright smile.

"You tripped me!"

"You must be mistaken, Mr. Dunnels," I said. "Your shoe laces are untied."

He glanced down at them. "What are you doing here?" he growled, glancing between Hentie and me.

"We came to offer our condolences," I said, smoothly. "What about you?"

"Don't bother," he snapped. "She can't talk. That or she won't talk. Darn woman thinks she can..." He trailed off, clearing his throat.

"Thinks she can what?" Hentie asked, and Barkington let out a flurry of barks.

"Yeah, we'd love to hear the end of that sentence."

But Dale grumbled and walked off, half-tripping over his laces, stopping to stare at them, then continuing on, shoving his hands into the pockets of his horrendous green pants.

I checked the tree, and a thrill ran through me.

Emery was gone.

And I hadn't been distracted enough not to notice her walking toward the back of the house.

It was almost as if she'd vanished into thin air.

Thirteen

"WHERE DID SHE GO?" HENTIE ASKED, scratching the bridge of her nose. "She was there a second ago."

Barkington followed Hentie's question with a bark and a doggy head tilt.

I checked the coast was clear, and that Dale Dunnels had actually left before walking over to the tree where Emery had been a moment ago. The grass at the base of the tree, between two gnarled roots, was flattened, but there was nothing out of the ordinary there. The black rose was missing.

I circled the tree and checked the surrounding woods, but they were quiet except for the chirp of birds or the rustle of leaves in the breeze.

She didn't go inside.

I was certain of it. I would have seen her, and there was the chance that my spy sense had dulled since I hadn't been on active duty, but no. No, I definitely would have noticed.

"Where did she go?" Hentie asked.

I brushed fingers across my brow. "She's gone."

"She must have gone back inside," Hentie said. "Ag, nee man. I didn't get a chance to invite her to Thanksgiving." Hentie opened the black purse she had slung over one shoulder, and fished around inside it, shifting Bark to her free hand. She withdrew a cute blue notepad and a ballpoint pen. "I'll leave her a note on the back door."

I followed Hentie onto the porch and waited while she wrote the note and tucked it under the mat, the corner peeking out so that it would be hard to miss but wouldn't blow away in the breeze. I strode along the porch, checking out the house. The windows were locked up tight, the curtains drawn, potted plants on the back porch were watered and green. The boards squeaked here and there, but overall, the place was looked after. Was that Victoria's work or Emery's?

This house was old, like Hentie's, and Victoria had taken pride in her family history and the town. It checked out that she would have cared for the home and maintained it.

"Ready?" Hentie called out.

I gave the windows either side of the screen door a final once over before joining Hentie. Together, we headed back to the truck and took the long drive around the lake toward Hentie's home. Since it was a short ride, Hentie let Barkington sit in her lap and enjoy the view until we got there.

Fifty minutes later, after freshening up, we sat down in the kitchen together to start prepping dinner and doing research about the case.

"Are you sure you want to spend your time doing this?" I asked, placing my laptop on the kitchen table.

"Ja," Hentie said. "It's a nice distraction. Besides, Blaffies loves a bit of adventure. Isn't that right?"

Barkington gave several enthusiastic barks.

"And I don't like sleeping in the same house where they found a body," Hentie said. "I don't understand how she got inside without being seen."

"She must have left and come back," I said. "Or she might've been caught outside the house and brought here. The best we can do is talk to the people closest to her."

"Emery," Hentie said, opening the Smeg refrigerator door and rooting around inside. "Ag, man, I don't feel like cooking. Tomorrow is Thanksgiving. I'm going to make a turkey. Can't we get some takeout?"

"I'm game," I said. "More time to focus on the case. How about pizza?"

Hentie ordered the pizza while I started my research. I had a suspect list in mind, but first up was a quick Google of the name "Victoria Dawson."

A Deep Dive on the Legacy of Prohibition in Texas

By Dale Dunnels, of the Society for Genealogical Research, Tickle Texas.

My adventure in Tickle first started when I moved to the town seeking answers about the reported warring families during the prohibition era in Texas. Rumor had it that two families, enemies since the inception of the town, had fought over moral, ethical and financial boundaries within the town.

I thought, perhaps, there might be some truth to the gossip, and my inquisitive mind couldn't stand not knowing the answer.

As it happens, the history of Tickle is much darker than its name.

During the prohibition era, the town was infamous for the production and distribution of moonshine, rumored to have been stored in homes, run through underground tunnels that spanned the entirety of the town beneath its lake. Now a tourist attraction, the Tickleton Lake, eponymously named for one of the town's founders Edgar "Tickle" McCulloch, is seen as an idyllic spot to relax and enjoy a refreshing beverage. The residents of

Tickle, blissfully unaware of the tunnels that run underneath it.

During the 1920s, when the United States government had prohibited the production and sale of alcohol, moonshine became the currency for Tickle and the surrounding towns in the county.

Two families were responsible for the production and distribution of the illicit alcohol. The aforementioned McCullochs, and the Dawson family. More about them later!

From my research, I discovered that both these families started out as humble farming families, keen to make their mark in Texas after leaving their respective homes in North Carolina and Oklahoma, hoping to eke out an existence in the state.

In order to do so, both heads of the families took on heavy debts. By the time the 1920s rolled around, they were almost out of options, and thus, turned to moonshine production.

"What are you reading?" Hentie asked.

I beckoned for her to read over my shoulder. "Written by Mr. Dunnels. Apparently, he's a genealogist. And he's doing research on the town and the families that ran it during the prohibition era."

"Oh, dis interrasant. That's interesting."

I returned to my reading.

The two families had an iron grip on the town, with incidents of violence breaking out between the families when lines were crossed. What had initially been a gentleman's agreement to work together on moonshine production—the patriarchs of the McCulloch and Dawson families had shaken hands on the deal in 1923—soon soured when the Dawson family began reporting the McCullochs for their illicit actions.

In an effort to find the truth, I reached out to two of the last relatives of Victor "Tall" Dawson who are still residing in the town, in the very house the patriarch lived in at the time.

Miss Victoria Dawson is a tall, stately woman with sweeping dark hair, rosebud lips, and a keen eye for anything that doesn't quite match her high expectations. When I asked her about her ancestors, those moonshine runners who had brought the town to the state of a small-scale war at the hands of the family patriarch, she was in complete and utter denial.

"My family was never involved in moonshine production," Victoria claimed, despite the evidence to the contrary. "We were upstanding citizens in Tickle. We didn't get involved in unsavory activities like that. My great, great grandfather, Victor Dawson, was a

preacher in the town and was elected sheriff after 1933."

I mentioned that the town's history pointed toward a connected tunnel between the Dawson and McCulloch abodes, but Miss Dawson didn't accept the idea.

"Those are rumors put forth by people who want to bring shame to our family crest. The Dawson family was never involved in moonshine. We were the citizens who stood against the moonshine movement during prohibition. The only family to do so."

Please find the image below which directly contradicts Miss Dawson's claims.

The image was a snapshot of two men, shaking hands, one with a cigar between two thick fingers, the other wearing a neat suit with his hair slicked back, and a wispy mustache above his lip.

The picture was captioned.

On the right, smoking a cigar, is Mr. Edgar "Tickle" McCulloch, and on the left, Mr. Victor "Tall" Dawson. They appear to be shaking hands in the midst of a deal. Behind them, a moonshine still is pictured.

And next to that still were several bottles, each of them marked with an 'x'

My eyes widened as puzzle pieces clicked into place.

The 'x' marks on Victoria's cheeks! That had to be a call back to the prohibition era. Even the way in which she'd died was related to alcohol. The direct injection into her system of the unfettered alcohol spoke of a revenge killing.

But who had done it?

Hadley McCulloch had mentioned, several times, that Victoria had wanted to ruin her fun, but was that enough for her to kill Victoria? The motive might run deeper than I realized.

Or could it be this genealogist, Dale, who had a temper and had been seen confronting Emery? He clearly knew enough about prohibition to have made those marks.

Secret tunnels under the lake.

"Hentie," I said, turning toward my friend, whose eyes were wide after reading the article. "Do you know who owned this house before Franklin bought it?"

Fourteen

Hentie tapped her nose. "I'm not sure," she said. "Franklin bought the house a few years ago. It's not his family home. The solicitor might have details. I can ask him for the deed and the information when we meet."

"There's a chance that this might be one of these homes." I pointed at the screen. "Prohibition era homes."

Hentie nodded enthusiastically. "What if it's the McCulloch house?" Hentie gasped.

"It could be. But where does Hadley live in that case?" It was possible that the family home had been sold, for whatever reason. People moved houses all the time, and it was more of an anomaly that Emery and Victoria had stayed in their family home without having moved on to another one or to another town entirely.

Then again, I was the type of woman who never gathered moss and that colored my perception.

The doorbell buzzed, and Hentie got up as Barkington released a flurry of yips and yaps. "That's the pizza," she said. "I'll be right back. Listen here, don't go adventuring without me. I can already see where this is going." She grabbed her purse from the kitchen counter.

"What do you mean?"

"You're going to go looking for secret passages, aren't you?"

I gave her an impish grin, and she returned it.

Barkington stayed with me as Hentie went to grab the pizza. She returned with the pie a few minutes later. "Pepperoni," she said, lifting the box.

"What's that?" I asked, pointing to a smaller white card carton on top.

"Fried pickles with ranch."

I laughed. I could barely concentrate on the food, but I hadn't eaten since the ice cream earlier. I wolfed my food down, barely tasting the tang of the pickles or the salt and savor of the cheesy pizza.

After a slice or two, I got up, wiping my fingers on a paper napkin. "I can't wait any longer," I said. "If this is the McCulloch house, I want to find out if there are tunnels underneath it. If that's the case, we'll have an entry point for Victoria and the murderer."

"But why would she come here?" Hentie asked. "Why use any tunnels at all to come to my house."

"It might be to do with the noise complaint," I said. "And she was suspicious of the truck. At the town hall meeting, she made a big deal out of us selling ice cream. She was convinced that we were lacing it with drugs."

Hentie rolled her eyes. "She was a special lady. So uptight for such a young woman."

Barkington pitter pattered alongside us as we moved through the house. I stopped at the base of the wooden steps that led to the landing and the two staircases leading in opposite directions.

"Not up there," I muttered.

"But the hidden room was up there," Hentie said.

"Yeah, but it wasn't linked to a tunnel, as far as I could see. It was a storage room. And the article mentioned that the tunnels ran under the lake. A connecting tunnel like that would start lower down. In the basement. Where's the basement?"

"This way," Hentie said, leading me through the expansive first floor, past a second living area, and then taking a sharp turn right at the end of the hallway.

A set of concrete steps led down toward a thick wooden door.

We exchanged a glance. Barkington ruffed under his

breath and pawed at Hentie's foot. She picked him up and soothed him with a few pets on the head.

"Jinne, I'm getting a bit nervous now. What if the killer is down there?"

"Do you ever go into the basement?" I asked.

"No. Not really. I haven't had a reason to go down there since I got back. I've been too concerned with Franklin's health and…"

His passing. I patted her on the arm. "Let's check it out." I walked down to the basement door and reached out, then stopped myself. "Gloves."

"Wat nou?"

"I need gloves. If the killer did come through here, I don't want to ruin the evidence by putting my fingerprints on the doors." And my latex gloves were squirreled away in my room upstairs.

"Ag, April, do you really think Remington is going to dust for fingerprints? They're already saying it's an accident."

"Better to be safe than sorry." I darted back the way I'd come, ran to my room, and grabbed two pairs of gloves. I handed one to Hentie and put mine on.

Hentie gestured with the gloves, flapping them around comically. "You have latex gloves? Little bit weird, April."

"What can I say?" I adjusted them with two satisfying

snaps. "I'm a germophobe." And then I opened the base-ment door.

It drifted ajar without a sound, revealing an unlit space, filled with boxes or covered items of furniture on a stone floor. Two things struck me as instantly suspicious, and I took a snapshot of the room.

Hentie took a step forward, and I cast my hand out to stop her. "Wait. Look."

A thin layer of dust coated the stone floor, proving what Hentie had said to be true, but several tracks made by different size shoes had been left behind.

Hentie gasped. "Someone *was* down here." Barkington gave a mini-howl.

I got my phone out of my pocket and took a photo so I'd have some physical evidence, rather than the image that was now tacked to the corkboard in my mind, a red line connecting the image to Victoria's body.

"There's something else," I said.

"Wat? What?"

"The door hinges are oiled. Not a single creak." I grabbed the side of the door and swung it open and closed again, demonstrating what I'd noticed.

"You're sharp, April. Maybe too sharp."

"Let's go."

Hentie and I entered the basement and followed the

tracks, walking either side of them, as they moved across the stone. They led us to the corner and a solid brick wall.

"Huh? It's a dead-end."

I traced my gloved hands over the wall, pressing against the rough bricks until something grated and clicked. The brick wall swung inward, grinding out dust from above that spattered over our heads.

Hentie coughed and covered Bark's nose.

I blocked my mouth with my arm, bringing my phone up and switching on my flashlight. The silver-blue beam sluiced down a long rough tunnel made of brick. Circular, the bricks were cracked in places, a few had dislodged.

"This looks like a building code violation," Hentie said, but she didn't sound nervous. "I'm going to put Barkington upstairs. I don't want him in any danger of a cave-in."

"No need," I said. "You two stay right here. I'm going in."

"But April, it could be dangerous."

"It's definitely dangerous," I said. "And that's why it makes sense that only one of us would go in."

"Ja, but you're young. You've got your whole life ahead of you."

"Young age does not equate to high value," I said, and stepped into the tunnel.

"Be careful!" Hentie hissed.

I gave her a quick, gloved thumbs up, then ran down the brick path. I wanted to make this as quick as possible to mitigate risk. The tunnel branched off in several places, some of those side-tunnels had caved in, some hadn't, but I kept on the straight main tunnel for now.

I'd come back in and explore later, when I was sure it was safe enough for both Hentie and me.

The tunnel was long, and I ran down it for ten minutes before I hit a thick-barred iron gate. It was slightly rusty, the gate itself a cut out in the center of the bars that spanned the circular tunnel from top to bottom.

I tried it, but the metal clanged. Locked.

The lock bore scrape marks, as if it had been used recently, and my heart thumped against my rib cage.

I took an image of the gate and its lock, and watched as a red thread zipped across my mental corkboard toward the painting of the key with Emery standing in front of it, her arms raised to the sky.

Just what on earth was going on in Tickle, Texas? What did Emery know about this key and this tunnel? And why had she painted a picture of it?

Was the key the stolen heirloom? Or had something else been stolen?

And did this tunnel end at the Dawson home?

Before I could piece any other clues together, a scream rang out from the direction I'd come.

Hentie!

Fifteen

I SPRINTED BACK AS FAST AS I COULD. FRANTIC
barks followed the scream. Bark was a yappy Chihuahua at
the best of times, but these barks were different. Alarmed.
Outraged, even.

The rough brick walls flashed past. Had I failed? I'd
been so concerned with solving the murder, I hadn't
stopped to consider that I was leaving her back there alone.
What if my enemies caught up to her?

I pushed on until the end of the tunnel came into
view. But Hentie wasn't standing in the opening any more.

Three steps later, I was in the basement.

Which was completely empty.

No. This is not happening.

"Hentie?" I called. "Barkington?"

Quiet and then, three faint barks from above.

I hit the button on the wall to shut the secret opening, the grind and grate of stone setting my teeth on edge, and then ran up the stairs and out of the basement. A low hum of voices came from near the front of the house, and I followed the sound.

"—nothing to be worried about." That was Hentie's voice.

Relief nearly knocked me off my feet. She was fine.

"Nothing to be worried about? That tunnel is a death trap. What were you doing standing in front of it?" Smulder asked, his tone low and suspicious.

Darn. He's onto us.

"I found it. Thought it looked interesting." And Barkington barked to back her up. Bless them. Hentie didn't know that Smulder was my spy babysitter, but she'd picked up on the fact that there was something going on between us, and that it entailed a lot of tension. She was covering for me.

"And the gloves?"

"I'm a germophobe. I was cleaning," Hentie replied.

"Where's April?" Smulder asked.

"Do I look like her keeper?" Hentie asked. "How would I know?"

"Is she in that tunnel? Be honest."

"Geen idee," Hentie said. "No idea. I haven't seen her since we finished our shift on the ice cream truck earlier.

Where were you, by the way? Weren't you supposed to help us?"

"I was otherwise occupied," Smulder said, and his tone took on a sheepish quality.

No doubt, he'd been getting chewed out by Special Agent in Charge Grant. Which meant I was about to get the same treatment from him. I glanced down at my clothing, dusted them off and removed the gloves. I was relatively clean—no evidence that I'd been in that tunnel.

But Smulder was a spy. I doubt I'd be able to fool him.

"You haven't seen her at all?" Smulder asked, skeptically.

"Are you saying I'm a liar, or what? Where I come from, we don't call people liars unless we have proof," Hentie said.

Barkington let out a low growl.

Smulder would never let a conversation like this escalate, but I stepped around the corner and into the kitchen anyway.

"Looking for me?" I asked.

His eyes narrowed as he focused on me. His gaze swept over my clothing and came to a rest on my face. "Been busy?"

"Not particularly. What about you?"

"Oh, I've been busy," he said. "On the phone."

Hentie's head swiveled as she took us in, and Barkington whined and placed a paw over his nose.

"On the phone," I said, meeting him stare for stare.

An awkward silence drifted through the kitchen, and I arched an eyebrow. "Is there a problem?"

Smulder's left eye twitched. "Can I talk to you in private for a second? Upstairs?"

"Sure," I said.

Hentie pulled a face at me, but I shook my head. I didn't need back up from her. I could handle Smulder and whatever came of this. I led the way to my room, but spared a glance for the end of the hall, my mind wandering to the moment I'd discovered the body.

I opened my bedroom door and stepped inside. Smulder shut it with a snap.

"I talked with Grandpa," he said.

"I figured."

"He's not happy."

"What else is new?"

"Can you take this seriously for a second, April?" he asked, irritably.

I turned toward him, folding my arms. "I am taking this seriously. I'm taking it deadly serious. I have no interest in having another argument with you about this. It's only going to end with us upset with each other and we're not going to achieve anything."

"I agree," Smulder said.

"You do."

"Yes," he said. "Grandpa knows that there was a death in town, but he doesn't know that it was a murder. I haven't talked to him about it in more detail than that. However—"

"You will if it comes to it. I'm well aware."

"No, that's not what I was about to say," Smulder took a breath. "I'm washing my hands of this."

"Huh?"

"Of whatever happens." He stared at me dead on, dark eyes fixed on mine. His lips were drawn thin. I hated that he gave me butterflies in my stomach when I was angry with him. "I've done my best. My due diligence. I have warned you. I have pleaded with you." His tone dropped low. "I've tried to protect you. I'm here to look out for you, but from now on, I'm not going to go out of my way to do that. I'm going to stick to doing my job. I'm washing my hands of this."

I nodded. "Fine."

The implication was deeper than just "washing his hands" of this particular case. He meant he was washing his hands of "us", though there wasn't technically an "us." There never had been, not properly at least. He was done with caring, maybe because he felt I didn't care enough for him, and that was fair and fine.

I could only do what I felt was right, and protecting Hentie and Bark was *right*. Smulder had come in as an outside agent.

I set aside the thoughts, festering and angry as they were, and lifted my chin. "Fine, Oliver." I used his code name. "I appreciate you letting me know."

He stared at me for a minute longer then turned and left the room.

I walked backward until my legs hit the wooden chest at the end of my bed. I sat down on it, pressing my hands to my knees and thinking hard.

My stomach was in knots, even as I tried to bring my focus to the board and the images on it.

The body. The evidence. That had to be my focus.

Victoria was connected to so many people and things in this town. Her family name was firmly ensconced in its history, and whoever had murdered her had used that history to mark her. But why?

I studied the images, thoughts of Smulder threatening to distract me.

There was the image of Hadley, red-haired, standing under the tree and talking to me conspiratorially, and then that fuzzy picture I couldn't quite make out. There was another shot of Dale Dunnels at the party, staring at Victoria who stood, dripping on the carpet. And then the sister, painting that ominous painting of the key.

The key I was sure fitted the lock on that gate.

But where did the rest of those tunnels lead? And what had happened to the key? Who was in possession of it?

The key might not even fit that lock, it might just be a painting that Emery had created because she'd wanted to.

But my gut said otherwise.

And then the mayor. The mayor standing on the podium with that long-suffering look on her face as she stared down at Victoria's ever-waving hand in the air. She'd been so done with her.

But had she been frustrated enough to murder her? And where had she been on the night of the murder?

"You push everyone away, Delta. You always have. You're such a mean-spirited girl. You should try to work on that. Nobody likes a mean girl." My mother's voice cut through my study of the board.

I was nearly sucked backward in time. I got up and left the room, determined to avoid those memories or the implications and feelings they brought with them. She didn't have control over me any more and she never would.

Tomorrow was Thanksgiving. Tomorrow was another day in which I could explore those tunnels and find out more about the house and what had happened, both in the past and in the present.

I went down to the kitchen to join my friend and her cute dog.

Sixteen

The following day...

THE THANKSGIVING PARADE WAS IN FULL SWING by the time we parked the ice cream truck down the street and hurried to get into position to watch the show. People jostled behind barriers that lined Main Street in Tickle, wearing smiles and waving American flags. Kids clung to their parents or sat on their shoulders, hopping up and down excitedly.

The people of Tickle loved Thanksgiving and they loved parades.

Personally, I wasn't a fan. Not because they weren't

fun, but because of the inherent danger presented by crowds.

It was easy for things to go wrong when there were a lot of people around, particularly if those people were obscuring you from seeing the bad actors among them.

Hentie and I took a place near the front of the barricade, squeezing in beside a family of four. A boy and a girl, both with wavy dark hair, hung on the railing, asking questions of their mother and father at an incessant speed.

"—a mermaid, Mommy?"

"That's what they said," the mother replied, shooting us a smile.

Hentie returned a grin, and I nodded. We'd left Barkington at home. This amount of people would either excite him or stress him out. Besides, we had a full Thanksgiving lunch planned, and the turkey was already prepped and ready to go in the oven. Hentie had secreted it in the fridge in case Barkington got any wise ideas.

"But I want to see the football team!" the young boy cried. "Are they going to have the football team?"

"Yes, honey."

"Can we have cotton candy? Is there cotton candy?" The little girl tugged on her father's jeans, and he scraped his hand through his hair.

At times, I'd pictured myself having kids—in moments

of weakness—but I couldn't say that I'd be a good mother. Especially not given my line of work.

"Here they come!" Hentie clapped her hands.

It was cooler today, but even with a nip in the air, the atmosphere was electric. It felt like good old-fashioned fun, and it was difficult not to get swept up in the excitement.

I scanned the crowd around us and across the street. It was dangerous being here, irresponsible even, but Hentie would've been suspicious if I'd refused to come along, and there was always the chance that we'd spot nefarious activity while we were out here.

The high school band paraded by, playing trumpets and wearing their band gear, complete with tasseled hats, and the crowd clapped and cheered. Next came the football team on the back of a float shaped like a football, the star quarterback standing at the pinnacle of the float, holding a trophy aloft.

"There they are!" The kids went wild, clapping and stamping their feet.

After that, came a Thanksgiving turkey float, driven by a grumpy looking guy, his tan arm hanging out of the window of the truck the float had been placed upon.

Colors and sounds dominated the morning as the local sheriff's department paraded by. The cheers were less pronounced for them than they'd been for the other floats.

Sheriff Remington wasn't in or around the float, only a few deputies there as representatives as well as the county mascot—a man in a bobcat suit complete with a police hat.

"There! The mermaids!" The little girl's squeal was followed by frantic clapping.

A glistening float appeared. The gorgeous mermaid, cresting the rock, her face turned toward the sun. On the back of the truck bed, sitting on the mermaid's tail, were Hadley and several other women dressed in shimmering tails of different colors and wearing crowns or tiaras.

They waved at the crowd as their float drove by.

I had to hand it to her, she'd done a great job at fixing the float on short notice. Nothing was out of place, and—

An awful creaking noise interrupted the music playing through the stereos from the passing floats.

"What was that, Mommy?" The girl opened her arms, demanding that her mother lift her up.

"I don't know. It sounded like—"

The float jerked forward, the driver grimacing in the cabin, and the stereo cut out as the truck slowed to a still.

Hadley, whose sparkling lips had been parted in a beautiful smile, whipped her head around, her red hair flowing down her shoulders. "Hey," she yelled. "What's going on down there?"

The driver yelled something back, but it was lost in the noise of the crowd.

"Yay! The mermaids stopped right in front of us. Can we go talk to them?" The girl turned in her mother's grasp, her pudgy arms outstretched toward the float. "I'm going to be a mermaid too. I'm going to be a mermaid when I grow up."

"You were a mermaid for Halloween, honey," the dad grumbled.

"Roger," Hadley barked, her grin fixed now. "Can you get the darn thing up and running? We're holding up the line."

And indeed, the rest of the parade floats had stopped behind the giant mermaid. Heads turned up and down the line of barricades, curiosity feeding the crowd with whispers and nudges.

"Roger!"

"I'm doing my best here," the driver snapped back. "Darn thing won't start. Just gave out or somethin'."

"You're kidding me," Hadley said, still talking through her smile, which was, frankly, scarier than if she'd shown her anger. "Did you fill up with gas like I *told* you to, Roger?"

"What do you think I am, dumb?" Roger countered.

Hadley shifted, looking as if she wanted to rise from

her seated position, but with that tail on, I doubted she'd get far.

"Wat gaan aan? What's going on?" Hentie murmured.

"No idea. But it doesn't look good."

And then there was a terrific groan and the screech of metal. The snap of wood.

Gasps and screams cut through the festive mood as the head of the mermaid, so perfectly painted, fell off and struck the roof of the truck with a terrific thud.

Hadley's jaw dropped. The other mermaids screamed.

The head dropped sideways off the top of the truck and hit the street. It rolled at a speed, directly toward the barricade.

The barricade behind which stood the little boy, grasping the railings as he stared at the truck and the mermaid and the chaos unfolding.

"Jimmy!" his mother screamed.

I grabbed hold of the back of the boy's shirt and whipped him out of the way, tumbling over backward and holding him to my chest as the head crashed into the barricade and rolled over the spot he'd been seconds before.

The mermaid's smiling face came to rest against a store, rocking back and forth before settling.

I got up, helping the boy to his feet.

His father reached for him, and I handed him over.

"Thank you," he said, blue eyes wide. "Thank you. You saved—"

"Don't mention it." And I meant it. I didn't want my name or face in the papers.

I turned to Hentie. "Are you good?"

She squeezed the messy bun atop her head and gave a quick nod. "That was scary."

Already, sirens whooped in the street and deputies who had been standing near the barricades had come through the opening to investigate what had happened and check if anyone had been hurt.

"Jinne, April, you saved that boy. He could have been crushed."

"Let's get out of here," I said.

"But it just started," Hentie replied.

My gaze flickered to Hadley, where she sat staring at the decapitated mermaid head, utterly shocked.

"Yes," I said. "You're right. But I doubt it's going to start up again anytime soon. I need to think." And I needed to get out of this crowd. Smulder hadn't told me *not* to come, but he'd looked on in disdain as we'd left this morning.

And he'd been right. This was too risky.

"I'm going. Do you want to stay?" I scanned the crowd.

Across the street, a man in a pair of sunglasses leaned

against the brick wall of one of the stores. He wore a t-shirt and jeans, his arms folded as he watched the chaos unfold, his expression blank.

The hair on the back of my neck stood up. I stepped deeper into the crowd and faced away from the street.

"April?" Hentie asked, catching up to me. "Wat's vout? What's the matter?"

"I have to go," I said. "Now."

Hentie shot a glance over her shoulder. "Then let's go. We'll get everything ready for Thanksgiving." Her voice hitched. "You look nervous."

"Not nervous," I said. "But the faster we get out of here, the better."

I started walking, checking the spot where the man had been positioned. But he was gone.

Seventeen

We made it home without being followed. The streets were clear as I directed us toward Hentie's house, but I couldn't shake the feeling that the man in sunglasses had been bad news. What were the chances that the head of the mermaid float detached like that, and right at that moment too?

I doubted that enemies of the country and certainly no one in the employ of the Crown Prince of Dubai would try to kill me with a decapitated mermaid's head.

Could the float have been sabotaged? And if so, why?

The only people who might have wanted to sabotage the float were the Dawsons. Victoria specifically. Had she done that before she'd passed? Or was this someone else? And if so, why?

I parked the ice cream truck outside the house, and Hentie and I headed inside, up the creaking front steps.

"Time to get started on Thanksgiving lunch!" Hentie rushed into the house.

Barkington came tippy-tapping into the foyer and gave us several barks in greeting. Hentie swept him into her arms and cuddled him tight.

I shut the door and locked it.

Smulder had a key if he needed to get in, and it paid to be careful, especially now.

"Come on, April." Hentie beckoned, and I followed her down the hall and into the kitchen. "You can start peeling potatoes for the mash. I'll get to work on the turkey. You know, where I come from we don't have Thanksgiving or turkeys. We make roast chicken."

"Still good," I said. "And easier to make."

"This is my first time making a turkey," she said. "But don't worry, I'm following a lekker recipe I found online. It's going to be delicious."

"I trust you."

Hentie set Barkington down at the kitchen table in his favorite chair then washed her hands and put on an apron. I did the same, and started peeling potatoes in the kitchen sink, frowning, my gaze lifting to the windows and the view of the sunny backyard. The clock ticked away on the kitchen wall as we worked, Hentie humming along to songs on the radio.

She brandished a turkey baster at me. "See? I came prepared."

And the murderer had come prepared too. With alcohol and a syringe. But why the cigarette? And who smoked in town?

"Sjoe. I can tell your cogs are working. What's going on in that head of yours, April? Why did you want to rush out of there so quickly?"

"It's got to do with the stuff I can't tell you," I said.

"Oh, okay, ja. That makes sense. The parade was so nice until that mermaid head made a bid for freedom."

"We are in the land of the free," I murmured, picking up a potato and starting on it. "Did you see the sheriff at the parade?"

"Nee. No. I didn't see him there. And I didn't see the mayor either, but I heard she was going to be on a float further down the line," Hentie said.

"Huh."

"What's up?"

"I'm wondering who would have wanted to sabotage the mermaid float and why," I said.

"Ja, and what about the tunnels under the house? What do you think of those?"

"I think we need to explore them. And talk to the suspects in this case," I said. "Should be easy since the papers have published that this was an unfortunate accident."

"You know what, April? These are not the right kinds of thoughts for Thanksgiving Day! Let's try to have fun while we can. I'm sure everything's going to be fine. We'll figure it out."

"But you locked the basement door, right?" I asked.

I was pretty sure that the murderer had come through that gate.

"It's locked." I let out a breath. "Then we—"

The doorbell rang from the foyer, and I brushed my hands off on my apron. "I'll get it!"

"Ooh! You sound just like an American movie." Hentie laughed.

I had no idea what she meant, but I jogged out of the kitchen and toward the door, astounded that Barkington hadn't launched into a flurry of barks the minute a guest had arrived. I looked through the peephole and smiled.

Not the guest I had expected, but I was happy she'd come.

I unlocked the door and opened it. "Hi, Emery," I said. "Nice to meet you. I'm April." I presented my hand.

Emery, pretty, with blue eyes and that dark hair, glanced down at the tips of her sneakers and then met my gaze with a small smile. She shook my hand, grasping only the tips of my fingers in hers, grip delicate.

"Come on in. I'm so glad you could make it."

I shut the door and locked it again, heedless of how it might seem alarming to her, especially since she'd just lost her sister. She'd come, and that meant we could get answers out of her.

I took her coat, hung it on the rack beside the door, then gestured for her to follow me into the kitchen.

"Hentie, look who's here."

"Emery?" Hentie spun toward her. "Ooh, wonderlik! Welcome. Come sit down. Do you want something to drink? A glass of wine? Can of Coke?"

Emery opened her mouth and shut it again.

"Sorry, liefie," Hentie said. "I forgot you can't talk. Do you have a phone so you can write your answers down in your notes app or do you want a pen and paper?"

Barkington gave two little yaps of greeting, and Emery smiled at the caramel-colored pooch, shyly. She swallowed, and studied the kitchen.

I returned to my spot at the sink to continue peeling potatoes.

"Listen," Hentie said, "we are very sorry for your loss."

"We didn't want you to be alone on Thanksgiving." I tapped the potato peeler on the edge of the sink.

"Thank you," Emery breathed.

Hentie gasped. "Oh goodness. Goodness, I didn't know you could talk."

"I can talk," she murmured. "I don't have anything useful to say."

"I doubt that," I said. "Would you like something to drink?"

"A Coke would be nice."

I got it for her, popped the tab and placed it on the table. Then I returned to my potato peeling duty. I wanted to give her room to breathe before I started asking questions. Hentie continued humming and making idle conversation. Barkington occasionally barked to join in, and Emery smiled.

"Thank you for this," she said quietly. "I don't usually get invited to go anywhere."

"Why not?" Hentie asked.

I'd moved on to chopping the potatoes up so they'd boil quicker.

"I prefer to spend time by myself with my art. And, also, when Victoria... when she was alive, she never wanted me to go out alone."

"Oh," Hentie said. "Why do you think that was?" She was so conversational, that it didn't sound unnatural to ask the question.

Emery shrugged. "She was worried about us being

attacked or that I would get in trouble. She... She liked to be in control of everything. Even me."

I kept my expression passive as I chopped potatoes and delivered them into a pot of water.

"But she wasn't a bad person," Emery finished.

"Of course not," Hentie said. "People are just people. Everybody has their flaws and makes their mistakes, as long as you end up doing the right thing, that's all that matters."

Emery took a few sips of her Coke. "I guess."

We continued cooking and the afternoon wore on. The later it got, the more delicious the kitchen smelled. Emery opened up, talking louder than she had when she'd first arrived and becoming animated.

Once the food was prepped and cooking, I sat at the kitchen table with her. "A toast," I said, raising my glass of wine. "To a happy Thanksgiving. And to Hentie's first official attempt at a turkey."

"Wish me luck," Hentie said, peeking through the oven door at the bird.

"Let's say what we're thankful for," I said. "I'm thankful for my good friends in Tickle and good company."

"I'm thankful for my friends and the food we're going to eat today," Hentie said. "If I don't make the turkey too dry."

Emery laughed, a musical laugh. "I'm thankful," she said, "that I got to see my sister before she passed away."

"You did?" Hentie asked. "What do you mean, liefie?"

"On the night it happened. I—I saw her at the house. She came back so angry, her clothes wet, and she, well, wished me good night. She said that she loved me, and that she would protect our family. And then I went to bed." Emery swallowed. "I'm grateful that I got to hear those words from her before she passed."

We toasted to her and to Victoria, and I took a mental image of her as she sat there, drinking to her sister's memory. The last person to have seen her alive.

Eighteen

A few days later...

EMERY DIDN'T REALIZE HOW MUCH INFORMATION she'd given me with her toast. Over the past few days, I'd been poring over the details in my mind, studying the corkboard and the connections between the images.

Knowing that Emery had been the last person to see her sister alive, or so she thought, meant that she was a suspect. It also meant that Victoria hadn't doubled back to the house on the night of the murder, and that she had gone home. It was plausible that she had used the tunnels connecting the houses, assuming that the connection ended at the Dawson home.

I sipped my coffee in the kitchen while Hentie bustled around, cleaning up the remains of our breakfast—she had insisted on cleaning up though I had offered, since it kept her hands and her mind busy.

"He's going to be here any minute," Hentie said. "Ag, I'm so nervous. Why am I so nervous?"

"Maybe because hearing from him will be like a final goodbye?"

Hentie stopped, wringing the end of her kitchen apron between her hands, eyes welling up. "I think you're right," she said. "I haven't been as focused on Franklin's passing over the last couple of days, what with the mystery, and Thanksgiving. I—I'm afraid to let him go."

"You don't have to let him go, Hentie." I got up and gave her a hug. "He'll always be with you. In your heart and your memories, and he'll be watching over you."

"Thank you," she said. "Ag, jy is te oulik. You are too nice." She patted me on the back and dried her tears on the ends of her apron. "I'm being silly."

"You aren't."

"Most people would think that my relationship with Franklin was strange, especially since we hardly ever spent time together, at least not face-to-face."

"It doesn't matter what other people think. You were happy."

"We were," Hentie said, then hesitated. "Most of the time."

The doorbell rang, and Barkington let out several furious barks from where he sat in his favorite chair at the head of the kitchen table. Hentie picked him up, her eyes widening. "That's him. The solicitor."

I walked through to the foyer with my friend and watched as she let in the solicitor, greeting him with a hug. Barkington gave the man a suspicious growl, but the solicitor wasn't fazed.

The man was short, with neatly combed black hair in a side part, bushy eyebrows, and a sharp, unblinking stare. He reminded me of an owl, especially since he'd chosen a tight-fitting cotton shirt to pair with his black suit jacket.

"Thank you for meeting with me, Mrs. Cooper," he said. "It's nice to put a face to the voice."

"You too, Mr. Huber. This is my friend, April Waters."

"Lovely to meet you," I said.

We shook hands. The man had an iron grip and a matching disposition. Hentie led us through to the living room where we took our seats.

"You're happy to discuss private matters in front of Miss Waters, I presume?" Mr. Huber asked, placing a black leather briefcase on the coffee table. He popped it open and removed several papers from within, patting them into order on his knee.

"Ja, of course," Hentie said.

Mr. Huber cleared his throat. "All right. Then let's begin. Your husband was generous in his will. He left money to causes that he cared about and to the people he loved."

"People?" Hentie frowned. "But Franklin didn't have any kids."

"No, he did not. Allow me..." The solicitor lifted the papers, cleared his throat twice, and then began reading. "To my wife, Hentie Cooper, I leave my newly purchased home in Tickle, Texas, to the value of two million dollars, including the land upon which it rests, as well as the sum of fifty million dollars. He has also left you a sealed envelope with a private message. To the Humane Society of the United States, I leave thirty million dollars."

My heart pounded in my chest. That was a lot of money. Life-changing money. I couldn't help but feel overwhelmed for my friend.

She can use it to hide and protect herself. See? She doesn't need you after all.

Hentie's jaw had dropped. She grabbed hold of her thighs and squeezed them tight. Barkington whined and licked her arms, trying to comfort her.

"Now, Mrs. Cooper, this last part may be difficult for you to hear. I apologize in advance, but you weren't the only woman whom Franklin mentioned in his will."

"What?" Hentie blinked, leaning forward.

Mr. Huber cleared his throat and refocused on the pages in front of him. "In addition, Mr. Cooper has left ten million dollars to Miss Victoria Dawson with a sealed envelope containing a private message for her as well."

I wasn't often stunned, but this news left me speechless. Hentie gasped.

"No, what? Why?" she whispered. "This can't be possible. Franklin and... Franklin and Victoria?"

"I don't know, Mrs. Cooper. I only know what's in his will." And then he stashed the papers into his briefcase. "The money has been transferred to a trust which you have full access to, of course. As for the matter of the deed to the house, it will be—"

"I'm sorry," Hentie said, lifting a palm. "I need a moment."

Mr. Huber checked his watch. "Unfortunately, I have another appointment." He rose from his seat. "I'll be in touch via phone, if that's all right with you." He stopped and pulled a face, lifting the envelope for Victoria off the coffee table. "Do you know where I can find Miss Dawson?"

"She's dead," Hentie said bluntly.

"Oh! Goodness. Oh my."

"I think you should take that to the police," I said, resisting my urge to keep the letter. If the cops found out about it, we'd get in trouble. And the lawyer couldn't hand over a letter that didn't belong to Hentie.

Seems like Emery is about to come into a lot of money.

"The police," Mr. Huber said. "All right. Yes, I'll do that. Have a good day, Mrs. Cooper. I'm sorry for your loss."

She stared at him blankly.

He cleared his throat and hastily left the room. The door shut a second later, and the silence spread. A grandfather clock ticked in the corner. What was with this darn house and all the clocks?

"Hentie?"

"Hmm."

"Hentie, are you all right?"

"I don't know. Why did he leave her money?" Hentie asked. "Why did he leave the woman who died in my house—" She broke off and shut her eyes. A second later, they snapped open. Her fingers fumbled with the envelope. She opened it, removed a letter and unfolded it, then began reading.

Hentie's face slackened, her eyes flicking back and forth. Barkington peered at the page, like he could decipher what it said.

I waited patiently.

When she was done reading, Hentie thrust the page toward me. "Read it," she said.

I took it from her.

Dear Hentie,

If you are reading this, then I have passed on. I want to thank you for the time we spent together as friends, and as husband and wife. I cherished our time together. You are an important part of my life.

However, there are things you should know, now that I'm gone.

Because of the nature of our relationship, and your desire to travel and see the country, I have been unfaithful in our marriage. I believe this is because I have always needed more attention than the average man. It's not a reflection on my love for you, only your unwillingness to provide me with what I deeply desired in our relationship.

I hope you can find it in your heart to admit this to yourself and to view our relationship for what it was. A beautiful thing. A purposeful thing.

One day, I hope to see you again, my love.

Yours,
Franklin M. Cooper.

I folded the letter and held it out to Hentie, but she refused to take it. I placed it on the coffee table and turned to her. "Hentie," I murmured. "I'm sorry. I'm so sorry."

"It was a lie," Hentie said. "Our relationship was a lie, and now, the woman he was having an affair with is dead. What's going to happen, April? What do I do?"

I didn't have any answers to give her.

Nineteen

THE ONLY THING I COULD DO TO HELP HENTIE, apart from moral and emotional support, was to figure out how the crime had taken place and who had killed Victoria. With the news that the younger woman had been having an affair with Franklin, another piece of the puzzle had clicked into place.

If those tunnels connected the houses, Victoria knew them well and had used them to liaise with Franklin.

Hentie was in no mood to leave the house or do any exploration. She'd retired to her bedroom to seethe, but only after I had asked her for directions to the suspects' houses. In return, she'd drawn me a map. I retrieved the basement key from a bowl on the kitchen counter and let myself into the basement.

I entered the opening that led into the tunnels and

began my explorations, writing the directions down on my phone. The first side tunnels ended in dead-ends. The third offshoot was longer, but had another of those iron gates, secured with a padlock that was rusted shut.

My footsteps tapped against the brick, echoing, and sweat beaded on the back of my neck as I walked. It smelled damp down here. Was I underneath the lake yet?

I examined the corkboard and its images while I walked.

The mayor who had called off the manhunt.

The suspicious Dale Dunnels who had written an article about the family.

Hadley, whose float had been sabotaged, and who had hated Victoria with a burning passion.

Emery with that painting of the key.

The house. Hentie had been so upset, she'd forgotten to ask who had sold the house to Franklin, and I didn't blame her for that. We'd have to find out when things had calmed down. When ownership of the house was transferred to her, she'd surely discover more.

The gate to the rest of the tunnel was locked tight. Whoever had taken that key, if my suspicions were correct, hadn't come back to the scene of the crime.

Dead-ends met me at every turn. Eventually, I started the walk back to the house. I had to act quickly. If I didn't, and news broke of Victoria's affair, the police might decide to look into the case with more fervor.

Time was running out.

And there was the stranger I'd seen at the parade to consider.

Tension stiffened my shoulders. There was too much on the line. Hentie's safety included.

Smulder's right. You should get her into that ice cream truck and leave.

But the cops would hear about it after the fact, and Thanksgiving was over. Sheriff Remington might start doing his job now that the pressure from the mayor had lifted.

I locked the basement door behind me then made a beeline for the exit. It was early afternoon, and I had my sights set on the suspects. Namely, one in particular.

Dale Dunnels had been looking for Victoria the morning after her passing. He'd been at the party, and he'd threatened Emery. He'd also written an article about the Dawson and McCulloch families. If he wasn't the killer, he might have useful information I could use to narrow down my list.

I got into the I Scream For Ice Cream truck, my mind whirring.

I brought my thoughts back to center and focused on the drive through town to Dunnels' house, but the more I thought about it, the more certain I became that the answer lay back at the Dawson mansion. The tunnels with their locked gate. The key.

Hentie's hand drawn map told me that Dale's house was deeper in town, further from the lake.

Ten minutes later, I parked outside a brick cottage with dusty windows on a back road in Tickle. Trees surrounded the house and birds chirped happily as I walked up the paved path to the porch.

The hair on the back of my neck rose, and I checked over my shoulder.

Nobody following.

But I had to be careful. Those strangers at the Thanksgiving Parade, coupled with the rogue mermaid head... Someone was out to get me, and I wasn't sure which entity these people worked for.

I knocked on Dale's front door and waited.

And then—

"Who's there?" The voice was close, pressed right up against the door.

I waved at the peephole. "Hello, Mr. Dunnels," I said, happily. "Having a good morning?"

"Is that a threat?"

"No. I was hoping you'd have time to talk to me today."

"Go away."

I cleared my throat. "Mr. Dunnels," I said, "I heard that you were a historian. I was hoping to talk to you about the history of Tickle. Particularly during the prohibition era."

A minute passed and then the door lock clicked. Dale appeared in the sliver between the edge of the door and the jamb, his hair standing on end. "What about it?" He looked every bit the crazed madman. Like he'd appear on TV spinning conspiracy theories.

Funny thing was, most conspiracy theories had a basis in fact, and as a Special Agent for the NSIB, I was well-versed in the cover-ups that took place in government agencies. Especially when it came to national security.

Dale scanned me from head-to-toe, his eyes narrowing. "You."

"Huh?"

"*You* want to know about history?" he asked. "You don't look like the type."

I grinned at him. "I'll try not to be offended by that."

He shrugged.

"I travel the country because I love finding out more about local history," I said. "I'm a collector of stories, you could say."

"Are you writing a book?" The door opened a crack more.

"Nope." I went with my gut instinct. Dale was the

type who enjoyed the spotlight. That article he'd written had been self-aggrandizing—my guess was that *he* was writing a book.

Dale sniffed, scrubbing at the end of his nose. "All right. Come in then. We can talk in my study." He held the door for me, and I strode into his house. It smelled stale, like it hadn't been aired out in weeks, with a faint air of wood polish.

Dale made a show of locking up then gestured for me to follow him.

We passed a living room with well-worn furniture and no TV, a kitchen that was cold and lifeless, and entered a study that was decorated with skulls. I arched an eyebrow, not because I was surprised, but because Dale would expect a reaction out of me.

"What's with the skulls?" I asked.

"These old things?" Dale turned and admired the collection—human skulls of varying sizes were stacked in rows on a bookshelf against the wall behind his desk. "I love finding skulls that have a history. Some of these are from the local area, others are from further afield. It's part of my work as a genealogist. You'd be surprised how willing people are to part with their skulls."

I opened my mouth to clarify then shut it again.

Dale laughed. "Oh, I see how that sounded. I meant

museums and other, uh, other places that display things of this nature."

"Right." I took a seat in a comfy chair in front of his desk.

The desk bore a computer screen and keyboard, as well as a much smaller skull—looked to be a rat—and a penholder. Dale snatched a pen out of it and started clicking away frantically. "You want to know about Tickle?"

"About the prohibition era specifically," I said. "I read this great article about the Dawson family warring with the McCulloch family, and I was fascinated."

"I wrote that," Dale said, tapping the end of the pen against his paisley tie.

"You're kidding. That was fantastic!"

Dale grinned. "I'm glad you thought so. Victoria certainly didn't. She was furious at me for publishing it. But then again, when wasn't that woman furious."

"I didn't know her," I said. "But it seemed like she had a temper."

"She was good at making enemies," Dale said. "Wasn't afraid of conflict. And look where she wound up as a result."

I pulled a face. "Poor Victoria."

Dale snorted. "She got what was coming to her. That

sounds disrespectful, but it's true. She believed that she was better than everyone else."

"I've heard she wasn't easy to get along with."

"Ha. Understatement. The day that article was published she egged my house."

"You're kidding."

"Nope. It was around Halloween, so she used that as an excuse to do it. When I confronted her about it, she acted like it was the kids that had done it. Just a regular part of trick or treating." He tapped his fingers on his desktop. "I knew the truth, but that didn't stop me. I've been writing a book about that family."

"I'd love to read it. Is it anywhere near finished?"

"Not yet," Dale said, his eyes shifting off to one side then back to me. "But I've got agents clamoring to represent me."

"Congratulations."

Dale puffed out his chest. "Yeah, thanks," he said. "What did you want to know about the prohibition era and Tickle?"

"In your article, you mentioned that the town had secret tunnels. Is that true?"

"Oh, definitely. Secret tunnels that span the underside of the lake."

"What did they use those for?" I asked.

Dale's eyes lit up. "For hiding moonshine, of course. A

few of those tunnels connected the Dawson and McCulloch households, and others contained secret rooms that held moonshine stills. It's fascinating really."

"But why would the families want to connect their homes if they had such a bad relationship?"

"It wasn't always bad," Dale said. "But I believe that they closed off the tunnel that connected them at years ago. Rumor has it, there was a key to the gate, and that said key had been lost many years prior. There were two sets, you see. One of the McCullochs and one for the Dawsons."

My heart skipped a beat, but externally, I kept my expression impartial.

Two keys meant two ways in. Was it possible that it had been hidden by a McCulloch ancestor years ago, never to be found again? Or was that second key with the killer? The first had been stolen from the Dawson's.

"That's so cool," I said, after a beat.

"It is, isn't it?" Dale bobbled his head enthusiastically. "Oh, I've been trying for months now to get those families to give me access to the tunnels under their homes."

"Are there no other entrances to the tunnels?"

"That's the work I've been doing over the course of the past few weeks. Trying to find entrances that aren't located at the McCulloch and Dawson residences. You see, the families had multiple homes at one point. I tried talking to Emery about the tunnels, but she played dumb as usual."

My mind zoomed in on an image on the corkboard. Emery underneath the tree near the lake, bending down. Rapidly, several other pictures flashed in my vision—Emery against the tree, hands up. Emery gone from the space in front of the tree. Rose on the ground at the base of the tree.

I stared past those images at Dale and smiled at him. "I wonder where those alternate entrances could be. Say, the house Hentie lives in, is that a McCulloch house? Do you know who owned it before Franklin bought it?"

"I think it was the McCulloch's." He sniffed. "But I moved here after that sale. And, like I said, there were multiple residences, so I can't confirm whether that's true. You might want to ask your friend."

But it was looking more and more like Hentie's house might have belonged to the McCullochs. I could ask Hadley, but if she was the killer, that might alert her to what I was up to.

"Don't you worry," Dale said, puffing out his chest. "I'm going to find the other entrances, and it's going to be easier now that Victoria's not around." He paled. "I—I— Ha, she was set on making sure nobody found out that her family had a seedy past. That's all."

"Sure," I said. "I hope you find those entrances." I rose from my seat. "I'll keep an eye out too."

"Great." But he didn't sound happy about it. He opened his top desk drawer and removed a pack of cigarettes. He tapped them on the desk, then removed a cigarette with a tan filter. "Are you attending the town meeting tonight?"

"Definitely," I said, snapping an image of him with my mind. "I'd like to hear what Sheriff Remington has to say about the murder."

"Murder. It was an accident, wasn't it?" Dale wet his lips.

I took a snapshot of him, the skulls arranged behind his head and gave a smile. "We'll see."

Twenty

Two keys.

Two keys meant that there were potentially multiple entry points to the crime scene. But the person who had killed Victoria needed to be connected to the scene, to have known about the secret room, and to have a key to the underground gate that was the way in.

It made sense that Hentie's house had either belonged to the Dawsons or the McCulloch family. Why else would they have been connected to these underground tunnels? But clearly, more than the McCullochs and the Dawsons knew about them.

Dale certainly did. And his article wasn't exactly secret. That meant most of Tickle had awareness of the tunnels and might have used them. And that was assuming that the other entrances hadn't been used to reach the crime scene.

Hadley McCulloch had moved up my list. More investigation was required.

Emery Dawson was another suspect who'd risen to the top. While Dale was suspicious, especially with those cigarettes, the sister had admitted to being the last one to see the victim alive. And she'd painted a portrait of the key. She'd appeared to be praising the thing.

That misty picture on the corkboard in my mind had cleared. I could make out shadows, but nothing else.

It was plausible that the key from the McCulloch side of the family had passed out of their possession long ago. And it was also possible that Dale was lying and had an ulterior motive.

I steered the ice cream truck around Tickle Lake. It was a chilly day, but the lake wouldn't freeze over in this weather. The early afternoon sunlight glimmered on the surface, and I couldn't help wondering what secrets lay beneath it.

The tunnels had been gated. Was it possible I'd missed something?

Instead of heading back to Hentie's house, I drove to the Dawson household, across from the Tickleton Observatory.

I parked in front of the house, then walked down the

side of it, my gaze fixed on the old suspicious oak. The location of Emery's miraculous disappearing act the other day.

But where was she now?

A door slammed in the house, and I crouched low, pressing the side of my body to the shiplap wall of the house.

Footsteps creaked on the back porch, and Emery came into view, her dark hair tied back from her face in a messy bun—she wore an oversized hoodie, and she pulled the hood up as she made a beeline for that tree.

I took mental images of her as she disappeared behind it. She bent and fiddled with something on the ground.

My eyes widened.

Emery tugged on the grass itself and a section thunked back on hidden hinges. She descended into the earth, reaching up to close the "ground" behind her.

I waited four breaths then got up and walked over to the old oak.

The section of ground where Emery had disappeared was nearly indistinguishable from its surroundings. No wonder I hadn't immediately spotted it. Whoever had created this trapdoor had done a fantastic job disguising it. The grass underneath the tree matched the "grass" on the trapdoor exactly, and had even grown over it at some points, adding to the illusion.

It was only after seeing Emery descend that I could distinguish a faint circular line in the ground.

I bent and felt around the edges of it.

There.

My fingers slipped into a wedge cut out of the door. A fingerhold to pull it up.

I did exactly that, exposing a darkened brick hole, complete with a rusted ladder attached to its side.

A tunnel that would lead under the lake.

What are you up to, Emery?

If she'd been aware of this tunnel, then my instinct about Victoria had been correct. She'd used the tunnel to get to Hentie's house. But how had the killer known? Unless it was as simple as it being Emery who had killed her.

I descended.

The tunnel was dark, the rusted ladder rungs cold against my palms. I descended, practicing my breathing, and listening for any sound of movement below.

At the bottom, I discovered a small outlet that led into a main tunnel.

A light bobbed in the darkness. A cellphone flashlight. Emery.

I followed her, keeping to the wall, feeling my way forward in the dark to avoid potential obstacles.

Emery's light stopped moving, and I caught up to her,

halting outside the circle of light. The wall dropped away to my left, revealing another offshoot, and I stepped into it, keeping back in case Emery decided to turn around.

My suspect was in front of a gate.

The gate.

The one that separated Hentie's house from the Dawson household.

This proved it. This *had* to be the way both Victoria and the killer had come.

"I wish you would have listened to me," Emery breathed. She tugged on the latch, testing it, as if afraid it might pop open of its own accord.

After a breath, she started back up the tunnel.

I intercepted her.

Emery shrieked and dropped her phone, light flashing over the bricks and her horrified pale face.

"Hi," I said. "What are you doing down here?" The phone had landed facedown, muting some of the light. I bent and picked it up, weighing it in my palm and then offering it to her.

Emery stared at me, her mouth agape.

"Emery?"

"W-Wha—"

"I asked you first," I said, with a bright smile. "What are you doing down here?"

"Nothing."

"Sure. Nothing." I considered incapacitating her, then restraining her and questioning her at length. I was on the brink of being desperate enough to do it. "How about you tell me the truth?"

"I—April, I was just coming down here to—"

"To check whether the gate that connects your house to my friend's house was locked?" I asked.

Emery began shaking so hard, the light skittered across the tunnel floor.

I brought my phone out and switched on my flashlight to even things out. "Your sister used this gate and the key to get through to Hentie's house, didn't she?"

Emery didn't respond but the trembling increased.

"Why are you checking that it's still locked?"

"I—I—"

I prepared myself, studying her body language. If she tried to make a run for it, I could stop her, but I was already crossing boundaries by blocking her exit from the tunnel. If she went to the sheriff... *He'll do nothing. Just like he's done nothing about solving this case.*

"Emery," I said. "I'm not going to hurt you, and I don't care about family secrets or legacies or any of that stuff. I care about helping my friend and solving this crime. Can you help me with that? Can you help me figure out what happened to your sister?"

Emery's shoulders drooped. "It's my fault."

"What?"

"It's my fault she's dead."

Was this a confession?

"If I'd thrown the key away sooner, it wouldn't have happened," Emery said.

"Sooner?" A piece of the puzzle clicked into place.

Victoria had been complaining about a stolen heirloom. Emery had painted that key, and almost seemed to be praising it. That part didn't quite add up, but the stolen heirloom? That had to be the key.

"Victoria used to... She used to use the key to go through this gate." Emery gestured over her shoulder. "She would take the tunnels to go and see her boyfriend."

"Franklin. She was dating Franklin." Poor Hentie.

"And I hated that," Emery said, her lips thinning. "I couldn't understand how she could be such a hypocrite. One second, she's freaking out at me for not giving a good enough impression of our family to the town, the next she's sneaking off in the middle of the night to go have an affair. It was disgusting."

"So you stole the key?" I asked.

"I didn't steal it. I threw it into the lake. Where it belonged. I made it look like a robbery. I thought it would put a stop to this, but it didn't. Instead she— She's dead."

"But if you threw your key away then someone else

must have let her through the gate," I said, piecing it together.

"I don't know who did it, but I'm sure they killed my sister. I just—I had to check that the gate was still locked, because if it's not then that means that they're around. What if they want to kill me next? What if they realize I threw away the other key and they want to get rid of me before I tell the cops?"

"Why *haven't* you told the cops?"

"I tried to," Emery said, pulling her hood down. "But Sheriff Remington wasn't interested. He kept waving his hand at me like it didn't matter and told me this was all an accident."

Because of the mayor. Who was also on my suspect list.

"This is important," I said. "If you want to find out who did this to your sister—"

"I don't."

"You don't?"

"No," Emery whispered. "I want this to go away. She was awful to me. She treated me like I was nothing but an add-on to her life. She mocked me for preferring to keep my thoughts to myself, but whenever I talked, she would tell me how dumb I sounded."

Memories from my past threatened to rise, and I forced myself to focus on the present. I fixated on Emery's throat, where her pulse hopped lightly against her skin. She was nervous. Coated in a thin sheen of sweat.

"I don't care if that makes me sound evil," Emery said. "The truth is, I don't care what happened to her. I'm glad she's gone." She turned and tugged on the gate's padlock one more time. "I just don't want to be killed next."

I hesitated. "Emery. Do you know who lived in the Cooper house before Franklin bought it?"

She frowned. "No," she said, facing me. "It was abandoned for years. I think it used to belong to the McCullochs, but they sold it, like, decades ago. Why does that matter? Why do you care about any of this?"

"I told you why. I want to help my friend."

"That's nice. Nice that you have friends." Emery drew her shoulders back. "Are you going to let me by?"

I stepped out of her path.

Emery was *not* clear. But there were other suspects to investigate.

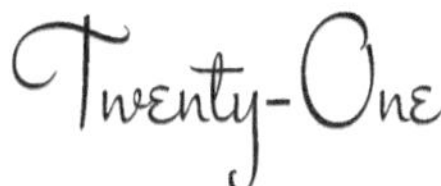

That night...

IF THE TOWN HALL HAD BEEN PACKED FOR THE last meeting, it was nothing compared to tonight. Folks stood around the edges of the room, murmuring to each other. It was hot, and I stood near the door so I could make an escape into the cool night air if I had to.

A couple of the attendees glanced back at me suspiciously, but they didn't come over. Hadley McCulloch stood in her usual spot at the wall. She tipped her chin upward in greeting, and I lifted hand in return.

Someone's cranky.

She had on a shade of pink lipstick today—not the red

that had been used to create the marks on Victoria's cheeks—and her mouth was turned downward at the corners.

I checked my fanny pack was in place—I'd opted to wear it after the sighting of a potential enemy at the Thanksgiving parade—and leaned against the wall.

Smulder walked along a row at the back of the town hall, and my stomach flipped. As he walked, women's heads turned to follow his passage through the crowd.

I didn't blame them. He was a good-looking guy. Maybe too good-looking to be an agent.

"Hentie's not coming?" Smulder asked, stopping beside me.

"She's keeping a low profile," I said. "And Bark is staying with her for moral support."

I'd messaged Smulder about what we'd discovered to keep him in the loop. As much as I didn't like having a babysitter, this was Smulder's career too.

"Sorry that happened to her," Smulder said.

"I am too," I whispered.

I didn't want to draw too much attention to what had happened to Hentie. News traveled fast in small towns, and the solicitor had been set on telling the cops.

Smulder's elbow brushed mine, but he didn't move away. He didn't smile at me either.

I sighed and kept my focus on scanning our surroundings for potential threats and assessing those gathered for the meeting. Everyone appeared on edge, and I'd bet anything that Hadley was angry about what had happened to her mermaid float. She stood clenching and unclenching her fists.

Mayor Barrera entered the hall from a side-door, accompanied by Sheriff Remington. The sheriff was red in the face as Barrera shook her head at him vehemently while she bore a fixed smile.

"Somebody's in trouble," Smulder said.

I didn't respond. He'd made it clear he was washing his hands and wanted nothing to do with me and my investigation, so why was he here? Doing his job reluctantly?

Not the time to worry about a man..

Mayor Barrera waved the sheriff away then mounted the steps of the stage and approached the podium. The room was small, no need for a microphone, but the mayor had to wait for the chatter to cease.

"Good evening, everyone," she said. "I'm glad you could make it to this impromptu meeting." Her lips thinned, and she glanced off toward Hadley. "Things have been a bit crazy lately."

Hadley snorted loudly, drawing gazes.

"But we've got everything under control. For those of you who weren't aware," the mayor continued, and heads swiveled back around to face her, "we've recently had two unfortunate events in Tickle. First, a beloved member of the town, Victoria Dawson, passed away in a regrettable accident."

Yeah. Surely it was an accident. I didn't let my doubt show.

Emery was notably missing. Dale Dunnels, however, was near the front, scooched right onto the edge of his seat, paying rapt attention.

"And second," Barrera said, "we had an interruption during our Thanksgiving parade."

"Is that what we're calling it?" Hadley said mutinously. "An interruption? A boy nearly died, Mayor. Are you kidding me with this?"

"Hadley, please." Barrera raised a palm. "This is a meeting, not a private discussion. Let's follow protocol here. I'll say what needs to be said, and then I'll open the floor to questions."

Hadley grunted and folded her arms. "Unreal," she murmured.

Whispers traveled through the room.

Barrera put up a bright smile. "Everyone, it's been a busy month. Let's take a breath, all right? I've been engaging with local law enforcement about the accident at the Thanksgiving parade, and Sheriff Remington and his deputies are doing everything in their power to figure out who sabotaged that float. Sheriff Remington?"

The sheriff came forward, looking years older than

when I'd last seen him. He dragged a hand over his jowls. "Yeah, we're doing everything we can. We've taken the float and the, uh, the decapitated mermaid head into custody. Once we have an update for you, we will release it so that everyone can get settled back into normal life in Tickle."

Barrera gave an awkward laugh. "Not that things aren't normal," she said, blinking rapidly at the sheriff. "Things are exceptionally normal."

"Exceptionally," Remington echoed the sentiment.

"That's a little on the paradoxical side, don't you think?" Smulder breathed.

I bit back a laugh.

"Can we ask our questions now?" Hadley said, her hand snapping into the air so fast that it nearly knocked the glasses off the man standing beside her.

Barrera pursed her lips and nodded. "Yes, I'll open the floor to questions."

"What do you mean by 'you have it in custody'?" Hadley asked. "Are you taking fingerprints? Sending it to a forensic lab?"

"This isn't *CSI: Miami*, Miss McCulloch," Remington replied. "It's a float. We can't send it off somewhere for testing. We're working within our agency to resolve—"

"And what about Victoria?" Dale called that out. "Is her accident being investigated?"

"I'm unable to comment on that at this time," Remington replied.

"He means no." The mayor stepped forward, putting a hand out in front of the sheriff. "There's nothing to investigate. An accident is an accident."

"But I heard that she was having... an affair with Franklin Cooper." That came from a woman near the back. "Doesn't that mean that Mr. Cooper's widow should be a suspect?"

"It was an accident," Mayor Barrera repeated. "Correct, Sheriff Remington?"

"I'm unable to comment on that at this time."

"Yes, you are," Barrera said, then turned to the crowd, her cheeks pinking. "Yes he is. There's nothing to investigate. Nothing untoward happened, so how about we all relax? Things seem a bit crazy, but that's just the nature of the holiday season."

"It's not even the holiday season yet," another person cried.

"That's not true. They've got lights up in the General Store. And a Christmas tree! Can you believe that? It's not even December." The man next to Hadley leaned forward.

"I heard them playing Christmas music." A shout from a woman, both shocked and horrified.

The questions grew in pitch and frequency. People rose from their seats, trying to get closer to the front.

"I'm afraid that's it for today," Mayor Barrera called. "Meeting adjourned!"

Groans and shouts rang out, but the mayor was already making her escape. She beckoned for Remington to accompany her.

Before Smulder could stop me, I slipped out of the town hall to follow them.

Twenty-Two

I MOVED AROUND THE SIDE OF THE BUILDING, keeping to the shadows and heading down the breezeway that flanked the town hall. The doors along its side were closed, but the rumble of activity within penetrated the thick wood. Light from windows high up on the wall lit my path, but it was dim.

I preferred it that way.

Mayor Barrera's actions were too suspicious to ignore. Even Remington wanted to investigate—it was obvious from his body language and the argument they'd had before the mayor had stepped up to the podium.

Thanksgiving was over, so why go through the trouble of participating in a cover up, rather than investigating the case? Sure, it technically worked in Hentie's favor but we couldn't leave town until this was off our backs. There was always a chance that the cops would come after us if we did.

I rounded the back of the building and spotted two figures on the grass under a copse of trees. The town hall was situated on an expansive square of land smack dab in the middle of town, with streets running past it.

There was no way I could sneak up on these two without them seeing me.

Instead, I reached into my fanny pack and withdrew a tiny bud. The last time I'd used this item to tune into a suspect's conversation, it had nearly deafened me—but this version was new and improved.

I inserted the fleshy bud into my ear and removed a watch from my fanny pack that would control it. I strapped the watch onto my arm, then tuned the dial that was its face. This "watch" couldn't tell time. It helped me tune into conversations depending on direction and distance.

I fiddled around with it until Mayor Barrera's voice sounded in my ears.

"—care. Nobody can prove I was anywhere near the mansion that night. But the more you poke around, the more dangerous it becomes."

Near the mansion? I made a mental note of it, writing the words out on a sticky note in my mind and placing it beside my snapshot of the mayor on her podium in town hall, a long-suffering expression on her face.

"Dangerous for who?" Remington asked, sounding irritable. "For you? Is that what you're saying, Marisol?"

I took a mental image of them standing facing each other in the darkness. If that wasn't suspicious, what was?

"No, of course not," she replied, but her voice trembled. "Colton, come on. You know how hard I worked to get elected to this position. I'm not going to throw it away over an irritating busybody. Victoria annoyed me, yeah, but she annoyed everybody. This is not about me. Or you. It's about Tickle."

"If you cared so much about Tickle, you'd want me to find out who did this. Thanksgiving is over. The celebration isn't at risk any more!"

"There are different ways to care," Mayor Barrera said briskly. "I care about putting this town on the map. Think about it, Colt. The Tickle Observatory hasn't been used in years. We don't have much to offer by way of agriculture, and before I was in charge, tourism was at an all time low. We need to inject money into this town. And with Christmas around the corner? That's going to be our busiest time of year. People will come to Tickle for Christmas. We can make it so that our town is the major destination in Texas for Christmas celebrations."

"Is that what this is about?" Remington sounded doubtful. "Christmas?"

"Yes. What *else* would it be about?"

A hesitation. I glanced over my shoulder, checking that the coast was clear. Smulder hadn't followed me out because he didn't want to get involved.

"And this doesn't have anything to do with that article about the top 10 towns in Texas?"

"Huh?" Mayor Barrera cleared her throat.

"I read it online. The top tourist destinations in Texas. The one that comes out every year on TravelTexas.com? We were number ten this year. That's five spots down from last year."

Barrera sniffed.

"I'm right," Remington said. "That's what you're upset about."

"I'm not *upset* about it. That website is *the* resource people use when they visit Texas. We need to keep them coming back, injecting money into the town," she said. "We don't need them worried about whether they're going to get murdered here. Do you understand? We've got to keep people calm and happy."

"The election is coming up next year," Remington said. "For mayor. Is that it? You want to get re-elected?"

"Don't you?" Barrera snapped. "Don't act like you wouldn't be threatened at the prospect of losing your job."

"The citizens of this town elected me to do my duty," Remington replied gruffly.

At least he had a backbone.

"And what is your duty, Colton?" Barrera asked. "Is it to cause a panic? Or is it to keep the peace?"

"I—"

"This conversation is over," Barrera said. "Do the right thing. Forget about what happened to Victoria. It was a regrettable accident and that's all." And then she walked off, leaving Remington's shadowy shape beneath the trees.

Instead of returning to the town hall, the mayor strode across the grass toward the sidewalk and disappeared around the corner. Remington grumbled indistinctly.

I removed the plug from my ear and tucked it into my fanny pack, then hurried around the building and joined the stragglers leaving the meeting. A few of them gave me dark looks.

"She's friends with her," a woman whispered. "The murderer."

"You think Hentie did it?"

"Are you serious, Angelina?" the first woman replied. "They had an affair. Victoria had an affair with her husband. And suddenly, Hentie shows up and she dies?"

"But she seems so nice."

"That's what they say about killers. Charming on the outside, but on the inside..."

"I don't know."

"She's not even from around here. Who knows how they do things in Australia."

"Isn't she from South Africa?"

I ignored the conversation and walked toward the food truck, alert for any signs of an attack. I found Smulder waiting for me, his arms folded, back leaned against the driver's side door.

I didn't say anything to him and got inside. He hopped into the passenger seat.

"Do you want to talk about it?" Smulder asked.

"Do you?"

He laughed under his breath. "That's not what I meant, April."

"There's no point in talking about anything," I said. "You don't want to know, and I don't see how telling you will make a difference."

I considered what I'd discovered tonight to distract myself from the awkward tension in the truck's interior.

Mayor Barrera was desperate to protect her position of power. Remington wanted to do the right thing, which was good news, but the fact that the mayor was so fixated on keeping the peace was suspicious. Particularly when she'd mentioned being at the mansion that night.

She could only be referring to Hentie's place.

But what motive would the mayor have to kill Victoria? From what she'd said this evening, she wanted to make sure the town ran smoothly, not disturb it.

Unless...

Could it be that Victoria had had plans to run for mayor herself? There was a fixation on the mayor's part about the upcoming election. That would be more than enough motive to get rid of Victoria. And then there was the fact that Victoria herself had laid judgment on the mayor at that initial town meeting I'd attended. And she'd wanted to "clean up the town."

Everyone in Tickle had secrets.

I drove around the lake, occasionally glancing at it and wondering about the second key. Was there a second key? Emery was happy her sister was gone.

"April," Smulder said, placing a hand on my forearm as I put the truck in park.

"Yeah?" The light touch sent shivers up my arm that I resisted with all my might. I nearly sank into the memory of our kiss. A kiss that had been a mistake and would never happen again. Certainly not after the words we'd exchanged recently.

"April, I—" He stared at me, then withdrew his touch and unclipped his seatbelt.

I stared at him, waiting for him to say whatever it was he had to say.

"Nevermind."

"Of course," I replied. "Nevermind." I opened the truck door and got out, bristling at the fact that he would bother starting a conversation he didn't mean to finish.

I had more important things to concern myself with. I hurried into the house, darkened except for a light in the entrance to the kitchen.

"Hentie?" I called out.

A scream greeted me.

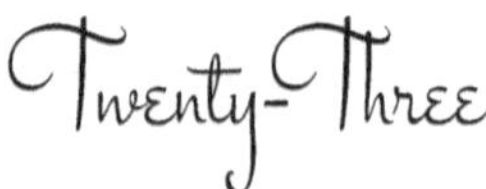

Adrenaline pulsed through my limbs, and I sprinted toward the source of the cry. My vision tunneled on the archway that led into the kitchen. Empty.

A flicker of shadow.

And then a masked and hooded figure appeared.

I bore down on them, maintaining my silence so that I could take them by surprise. But the figure noticed me and ran down the hall, heading for the basement.

The killer.

I skidded to a halt in the kitchen doorway to check Hentie was okay.

She was wide-eyed, standing at the counter with a knife in hand, potatoes on a chopping board in front of her. "Are you all right?" I managed. "Bark?"

Hentie nodded, her mouth opening and closing, wordlessly. Barkington howled from underneath the table.

Go!

I sped after the masked person, my heart pounding in my throat. They'd been average height, slim built. Not Dale then.

I took the stairs into the basement three at a time and vaulted over a covered chair. The figure was already in the tunnels speeding along, a flashlight in their hand the only sign of their passage.

Into the darkened tunnels I went, scrambling my phone out of my pocket.

Come on. Faster. Get there faster.

I pumped my arms back and forth, gaining on the person, but they were fast.

Thankfully, they ran straight down the tunnel, keeping in view.

Why?

The answer came moments later, when they crashed through the dividing door that separated the McCulloch tunnels from the Dawsons'. They'd unlocked it. They had the key. They had to be the killer.

I chased after them, crashing into the other half of the tunnels.

The figure took a sharp left and disappeared down an off-shoot, and I followed.

And ran straight into a brick wall.

The collision nearly knocked the wind out of my lungs. Pain flared in my wrist and my phone clattered to the brick floor.

I backpedaled, gasping and holding my hand to my chest.

"Darn."

This was impossible. There was no way they'd disappeared. Had I taken the wrong turn?

My wrist throbbed, but I ignored it, picking up my phone and directing the flashlight back the way I'd come. The tunnel was intersected by two off-shoots, the one I was in and another opposite it. Both were dead-ends and both were empty.

But the person I'd been chasing had definitely come this way.

I backed out of the tunnel and stood there, looking left and right. Nothing. Empty.

But how?

I walked down the main tunnel, checking the other tributaries that led off it. There was no sign of the killer. They had to be the killer. Because the killer was the only one who had the key to the gate, unless I counted Emery—who might've been lying about throwing her copy of the key away.

I grabbed hold of the bottom rung of the ladder that

led up to the trapdoor above, but winced. I couldn't climb it with my wrist. My gut said it was sprained.

Footsteps tracked up the tunnel, and I backed up, preparing for a fight.

Smulder came into view. "April!"

"Here." I flashed the light at him as I returned back to the area where the killer had disappeared. I entered the tunnel and studied the wall. There had to be a trap door or another switch that would open into a secret room.

I walked up to the bricks and pressed my ear to them, listening.

"April, you're hurt."

"Yeah," I said, as Smulder took the phone from me.

I backed away from the wall, frowning. "There's a trap door here. We need to find it. The killer must have used it."

"You're sure?"

"Pretty sure."

"But wouldn't you have seen it open or close?"

He had a point. The door in Hentie's house took time to open. I'd turned the corner fairly quickly after the hooded figure had disappeared. "People don't disappear," I said irritably.

Every minute that passed put more distance between me and the killer. Worse, they had been in Hentie's house. They'd come for her. Or for me.

What if this wasn't the killer? What if it was whoever

was in town, trying to hunt me down? *There's no truth to that. You're under threat, but a guy in sunglasses doesn't equal enemies.* And then there was the key to consider.

"We should leave," Smulder said.

"I don't know how else to say this," I said. "I can't leave. If I leave and Remington decides to investigate, my name will be in all the papers anyway." That was a certain way to get my cover blown.

"I meant the tunnel, April." And then Smulder took me by my uninjured arm and led me away. "You're not going to find whoever did this by standing there with an injured arm."

I let him lead me, simply because images had flooded my vision.

Gate unlocked.

Fleeing killer. Average height and slim build. Didn't match Dale Dunnels, but did that rule him out? Could be that he was working with the killer? Just how many people had wanted Victoria dead.

Hentie in the kitchen, shocked, thankfully holding a knife. I couldn't think about how different that scene might've been if I hadn't arrived or if Hentie hadn't been chopping potatoes.

The killer had returned to the scene of the crime.

But why?

Why would they have wanted to come back instead of

leaving town or lying low? Was there something in the house drawing them back? Or did they want to get rid of witnesses?

I scanned the corkboard, the connecting threads, and the blurry image. Shock thrilled through me. It was clearer than before. It looked to be a well-lit image. A single figure dominated the frame, but I couldn't make out who they were, where the image had been taken, or why it was relevant.

Smulder guided me into the house and locked the basement door.

How was it unlocked? Did I leave it that way? I would never have done that.

Hentie awaited us in the kitchen, her cellphone pinned to her ear and Barkington clutched in her arms. "Ja," Hentie said. "I'm still here. Are they coming or what?" A pause and Hentie caught sight of us. She covered the end of her phone. "I phoned 911. They're sending some deputies. Ag nee, April, what happened to your arm?"

Barkington barked, sounding concerned.

"I'm fine. I ran into a wall." Smulder seated me at the table and hovered over me.

My heart fluttered, but that warm feeling was replaced by irritation. I was a spy. I didn't need his protection. In fact, if he hadn't shown up, I would've been hunting down the killer. I would've found a way through.

"Tell them to send medical," Smulder said. "I think she's broken her wrist."

"Sprained at most," I replied.

Hentie nodded and talked to the 911 operator while Smulder dropped down in front of me. "I think you're underestimating your own pain threshold. Look down."

I glanced at my wrist and found that it was swollen to three times its normal size. "Darn." The pain got worse, but I practiced my breathing and ignored it, my gaze flicking back and forth as I went over the facts. "Secrets. Tunnel."

"April," Smulder said. "Not the time. Relax. The cops will be here any minute."

"And do what?" I whispered. "Riddle me that."

"They'll take care of the situation."

"Sure, they will." Smulder didn't know what I knew. Remington's hands were tied.

"You can't beat yourself up over this."

"I'm not beating myself up," I said. "I'm fine, Oliver."

"Nothing about this is fine," he replied, smoothing my hair back from my face. "I'm going to get you a glass of water."

"Would you stop babying me, please?" I asked. "I appreciate what you're trying to do, but I'm seriously okay. When the EMTs get here, they can handle it. For now, I need to sit and think." I lowered my tone, glancing off at

Hentie, who was on the phone near the kitchen windows. "Check on her. She needs it more than me."

Brian hesitated. Finally, he nodded and rose, but not before he pressed his fingers to my cheek. A final, soft touch that gave me goosebumps.

Darn him.

Focus.

The killer.

Average height.

Barrera was average height. That hoodie the killer had been wearing gave away their height and build but not anything else. It could have been her. If only the attacker had looked back at me. I'd have seen their eyes. That type of identifying feature would have helped.

The sabotaged float. The key. The mayor and the markings on the victim's cheeks. An affair. Prohibition. How was it all connected?

I smoothed my hand over my forehead. This wasn't getting any easier.

Twenty-Four

Smulder and Hentie had been separated, a deputy with either of them to take their statements. Barkington was tucked into Hentie's arm, his caramel colored head peeking out as he considered the deputies and the events unfolding around him.

And I was the lucky lady who got paired with Sheriff Remington himself. An EMT had already stabilized my wrist and given me painkillers. I'd been informed I was due for a hospital visit to dress my broken wrist.

An irritating piece of news since first, Smulder had called it, and, second, this was the last type of injury I needed.

The pain kept me angry, though. Angry and focused.

Sheriff Remington walked me through to the living room

and sat me down in a cozy armchair near the fireplace—unlit, though it was around that time of year. I drew my shoulders back and cleared my mind of thoughts as best I could.

I needed to be present for this. Hentie had officially been threatened, and I was going to stop at nothing to make sure this killer ended up behind bars.

Remington snorted to clear his throat, and I held back a grimace. "Miss Waters," he said. "Right?"

"That's right," I replied.

"We talked prior to, uh, Thanksgiving, if I'm not mistaken?"

"Yeah."

"How about you talk to me about what happened here today? Everybody's a little uptight lately."

The implication being that we were being uptight about an intruder? I struggled to give Remington the benefit of the doubt after the discussion I'd heard between him and Mayor Barrera.

"There was a masked intruder in our house," I said. "After a body was discovered upstairs. Don't you think that warrants a call to the police?"

Remington wet his thin lips. Sweat beaded on his forehead, and he removed a handkerchief from his pocket with much shifting and then swiped it over his skin. "Absolutely," he said. "You did the right thing. But I'd like you to tell me what happened. What exactly did you see? How did it go down?"

I gave him the rundown, going as far as to say that I'd chased the suspect into the tunnels underneath the house. The time for keeping secrets from the cops was gone. I wanted them to figure out what had happened. The sooner they did that, the sooner Hentie's name would be clear for us to leave.

Until this was solved, I didn't see how we could move on to the next town.

Remington made a couple of scratches on a notepad while I talked, using a stubby pencil that would've suited a server in a coffee shop rather than a law enforcement official. He glanced over his shoulder at the entrance to the kitchen three times during my breakdown of the events. Remington also scratched his ear, loosened his collar, and adjusted himself in the armchair repeatedly.

Uncomfortable.

"Got it," he said. "Got it. Thanks for giving your statement. We'll have our deputies looking for the suspect now." He started moving to stand.

"You don't want to go downstairs into the basement and see the tunnels?" I asked.

"That won't be necessary," he said.

"It won't be necessary for you to investigate the last place a masked stranger was seen?" I asked. "We just experienced a home invasion. No offense, Sheriff Remington, but I expected more from you, especially given what happened earlier in the week."

"That's nothing to worry about," he said.

"Right. It was an 'accident' as Mayor Barrera put it. An accident that involved lipstick crosses on a woman's cheeks and a secret room. She was injected with pure ethanol for heaven's sake. It was a murder, but you don't want to call it that." The words came out hot and barbed.

I was tired of this. It was ridiculous that nobody was doing a darn thing except for me.

And worse that you can't figure out who did it.

It was frustrating that law enforcement wouldn't take this seriously while Hentie's life was in danger, and worse, it was frustrating that I had failed to find the responsible party. That blurry image in my mind remained, taunting me on the corkboard.

Who had done this?

Barkington yapped from the kitchen, breaking the tension.

Remington pushed up from the chair, and I matched him, keeping my gaze level with his.

"You can't bury a murder forever," I murmured.

Remington's eyes widened. "What did you—?"

"It's obvious what's going on here," I said. "You want to do your job, Sheriff, I can tell. You're a good man. You look after the people in this town. Tickle would be lost without you, so why are you hesitating?" I'd inflated his ego purposefully there.

He froze.

"Aren't you worried about when you're up for re-election?" I poked at the potential sore spot. "The county needs a sheriff who takes action. I've heard a lot of rumors about you lately." A lie. But the citizens of Tickle weren't happy, if that town hall meeting was any indication.

"There's nothing I can do."

"You could investigate what happened to Victoria Dawson. Her killer is on the loose."

"That's—"

"Are you doing anything to make sure this doesn't happen again?" I asked. "Do you have any suspects?"

"Look, lady, it's not that simple," he said, glancing left and right then down at my injured arm.

"Emery Dawson," I said. "Dale Dunnels? Hadley McCulloch?"

"Stop," he hissed. "Stop it. You're not the sheriff. I am."

"Then act like it," I replied. "The person who broke into this house was likely the murderer, and you don't seem to care." A thought sprang to mind—I could narrow down my suspect list by establishing where the suspects had been during the time of the home invasion. "I have to go."

"We can give you a ride to the hospital," Remington said. "If you—"

"I have to make a stop at the Dawson household first," I replied. I was hoping to goad him into doing his job.

"There's no point," Remington called. "Nobody's home."

I arched an eyebrow.

"I've taken Miss Dawson in for questioning," he said, and came forward. "In connection with her sister's passing."

Ah. So he *had* decided to go against Mayor Barrera's directive. "When did that happen?"

Sheriff Remington hesitated then shook his head. "This is an open investigation. She—"

"Look," I said, drawing closer to him. "I want to know if she's the one who threatened my friend. Can you at least tell me that much?"

"It would be impossible for it to have been her. I took her in for questioning shortly after the town hall meeting," Remington said, and then he frowned deeply. "I love this town. I want to do right by it, even if it doesn't always seem that way. But I don't need you going around spreading rumors that we're covering anything up. That's..." He couldn't say it wasn't true.

His hesitation had me convinced that Barrera had played a pivotal role in the murder. But I had to rely on the evidence, not my feelings about the matter.

Could Barrera have gotten to the house in time after leaving the meeting? I stepped forward, moving my injured arm out of habit, and wincing at the pain. Darn. I had to get to the hospital and get this treated. The painkillers would wear off soon enough, and the adrenaline had already abated.

"Do you have any more questions for me, Sheriff?"

"We're going to take this seriously," he said, gesturing lamely over his shoulder toward the kitchen. "This home invasion. Don't worry. The sheriff's department is on your side."

Sure, they were.

Of the towns I'd been to, including one where the sheriff was a suspect, this had to be the most morally corrupt.

I exited into the hall.

Smulder waited for me near the door. "I can take you to the hospital," he said, his brow creased.

"Thanks," I said. "I'd drive myself but that won't be possible." I moved toward him then stopped and looked back. "I want Hentie and Bark to come with us. Or at least leave the house. There's a chance whoever broke in will come back."

Smulder nodded. "Of course. I think the deputy's almost done taking her statement. Maybe we should sleep somewhere else tonight. A guesthouse?"

"Maybe," I said, lowering my tone. "We'll secure the house and that will be—"

Smulder stepped into my space, close enough that his warmth and the scent of his woody cologne washed over me. He didn't touch me, but lowered his head and studied my arm closely.

I stared at the side of his face, my heart pounding wildly. This fascination with him was toxic and unnecessary. A betrayal to my ex, who had passed on.

"I'm worried about you, Delta." He breathed my real name, and goosebumps chased over my neck and arms.

"I can take care of myself."

I hoped those wouldn't be my "famous last words."

Twenty-Five

WE DROVE HOME WITH MY WRIST IN A CAST IN darkness, the truck's headlights beaming on the dark road that led back into Tickle. The hospital was in the town over and the drive there had been long, quiet, and painful.

Smulder was in the driver's seat, while Hentie had checked into a local guesthouse for the night. While we loved the massive old mansion, we'd had enough of the craziness. From the hidden rooms, to the tunnels in the basement, and now the invasion by the killer.

Who, notably, couldn't be Emery.

One suspect ruled out.

That was assuming the attacker had been the killer. But I didn't see another option. They'd had the missing key.

But how had they disappeared?

Brian cleared his throat. He was handsome, even in profile. "About earlier…"

"We don't have to talk about that," I replied. "Honestly, Oliver, I'm tired of the back and forth. Either you're interested or you're not."

"It can't be that black and white. You know it can't be, given our line of work."

"Why not?" I asked.

He sighed. "Because we can never— Look, our first priority will always be elsewhere, if you catch my meaning." He was worried the truck was bugged, hence the vagueness in his words.

We were meant to be committed to our country and protecting it.

"I get that," I said. "But I've learned a lot over the past few months. The past year." From the moment I'd been compromised and thrust into this new life. From spending time with Gamma and Charlie, losing Mickey, and then moving onto the truck and this life of traveling with Hentie and Bark, emotionally, I had never been through as much as this.

I'd spent years burying everything and it was all coming to the surface.

"Care to elaborate on what you've learned?" Smulder asked.

"That there's right and wrong," I said. "Maybe there's

gray area in between, sure, but for the most part, if you want to be something or do something, the only person standing in your way is you."

"You should be a motivational speaker," Smulder replied, and I rolled my eyes at his sarcasm. "I'm serious. That was deep."

"And you're avoiding the topic."

The sound of the tires on the road and music playing on the radio followed that.

"I don't know what to say," Brian said. "There's— It's a mess."

"Why?"

"Because I don't think you know what you want, and I certainly don't want to get burned again."

"Burned?"

"I—The last relationship I had ended poorly. It was amicable, but it still hurt, and it was—This is weird, but it was with your cousin." He grimaced.

I shrugged. "I figured. The way you acted about her when we first met tipped me off."

"Oh."

We entered Tickle via the main street, where the Thanksgiving decorations were still up, and the wrought iron lamps illuminated the quaint buildings that lined the paved sidewalks. I let the quiet grow between us.

"I don't want to get my heart broken again," Smulder said.

My stomach flipped. "Nobody wants that." The truth was, I was afraid to try. I was especially afraid of letting go and seeing the people I cared about in trouble because of me. Charlie and Gamma had already fled their small town because of my issues. And now, I was injured and couldn't even protect the people I cared about to the full extent of my abilities.

"Any idea who might be looking for me?" I changed the subject. It was pointless discussing it when it couldn't go any further.

Before Smulder could answer me, my phone trilled in the pocket of my jeans. I wormed it out with my uninjured hand and answered. "Hello?"

"April." Special Agent in Charge Grant's voice was gruffer than usual. "Just what in the heck is going on over there?"

"Nothing in particular." I glanced down at my broken wrist. "Why do you ask, Grandpa?"

Smulder stiffened beside me, but directed the truck toward the road that led to the guesthouse where Hentie was staying tonight—The Tickleton Guest House.

"I've received a request from your cousin, Oliver," he said. "He wants to leave his current position and return to living with me." Meaning that Smulder had put in an official request to give up his job as my agent baby sitter. He wanted to go back to being a normal agent with the NSIB.

I turned my head and stared at him.

Brian's neck had gone red.

My scalp prickled with anger. How could he? How could he pretend that he wanted to stay here and that he was interested in me when he wanted to leave? When he didn't even want to be here?

"I have no idea why that would be the case," I said. "I haven't done anything to upset my dearest cousin." The words came out bitterly.

Smulder winced. He mouthed something at me, but I ignored him.

I practiced my breathing and brought myself back down to earth. To the cold, calm collected version of Delta who wouldn't take this to heart. *Of course,* Smulder didn't want to work with me. I'd given him nothing but trouble, and he didn't like being around me. Whether that was because he had feelings for me, as he claimed, or because he wanted an escape was none of my business.

"You'd better be telling the truth," Grant said. "I'm getting tired of worrying about you, April. I'm starting to think it might be time for you to visit your friends down under."

"No," I said, quickly. "I think my cousin is just concerned about his future."

"Doesn't matter what he's concerned about. I've denied his request."

I shut my eyes. "You denied it."

Smulder was silent next to me. He'd brought the truck to a halt outside the guesthouse, but he hadn't left me in the truck to talk to Grant in peace.

"I have denied it," he said. "I don't have another friend to go on vacation with you." There weren't other agents he could spare to watch over me. "No one that I would trust to look after my favorite granddaughter."

"Aren't you sweet, Grandpa."

"Sweet enough to give you a toothache." Grant was deadpan.

"Are you calling me to tell me about my cousin's plans or...?"

"I have it on good information that our unwanted friends have moved out of Texas. Now is the time to run."

I perked up. This was good news. "They're gone?"

"From Texas, yes," he said.

But what about the stranger with sunglasses? Granted, he could've been a Tickler.

"You think we should leave while we have the chance."

"Correct."

Either the people looking for me were no longer in Texas, or they were hiding their presence much better. I'd changed my appearance enough over the past couple of months that I might have evaded them. "I wonder why that is," I said, after a beat.

"I have a feeling it might have to do with the rest of the family going on vacation. Regardless, you have two days to prepare your things and leave."

Charlie and Gamma had left Gossip and Texas. Could it be that their movements had drawn the heat away from me? It felt like this should be good news, but we weren't out of the woods yet. Literally. The guesthouse outside was ensconced between the trees, further back from the lake.

Two days, though. He expected me out in two days, and that was likely due to Smulder trying to back out of being my spy babysitter. Grant had to sense that something was seriously amiss.

Smulder might have protected the details of what had happened here, but Grant wasn't dumb. He was a Special Agent in Charge.

"Call me any time, Grandpa," I said. "I like our chats."

"I usually talk to your cousin," Grant said. "But I'll consider it. Two days. If you're not on your way by then, I'll send you to see your cousins down under." And then he hung up.

"Goodbye to you too," I muttered, and slipped my phone back into my pocket.

There wasn't a chance in heck I was going underground or leaving Hentie and Barkington behind.

"April," Smulder started, but I shook my head.

"I'm good," I said. "You were right. Too complicated. Too messy. Too much of a ridiculous idea. Nothing's as black and white as I thought, right? And you did what you had to do." And then I opened the door and slipped out onto the sidewalk, trembling from head to toe.

Was it wrong to be upset with him for this? Probably. He was just doing what he thought was right.

So was I.

I hurried toward the single story guest house. It was quaint, with a log cabin vibe, the curtains closed, but a flickering orange light in two of the windows beside the front door—a fire crackling in a grate. Smoke rose from the chimney. I couldn't wait to get inside and see Hentie and Bark.

And then, I was going to hunt down the last suspects on my list and solve this mystery.

The sooner we solved this, the sooner we could get out of state. Charlie and Gamma might've bought me time, but I couldn't trust that it would stay that way.

And I didn't want to think about what it would mean for us if the agents of the Crown Prince of Dubai found me. And my friends.

Twenty-Six

"En nou?" Hentie asked, perched on an armchair in my tiny room in the guesthouse. I had a single bed with a puffy white comforter and matching pillow, a couple of armchairs and an en suite bathroom. The wood walls were interrupted by a single window that looked out on the night sky. I stood with my back to the room, my hands locked together over my stomach.

I wasn't sick, just disappointed, and struggling to keep negative memories from surfacing tonight.

The only positive was that those who were after me weren't in town.

Two days.

I could do this in two days if I had to, but it might get messy. And I certainly couldn't involve Hentie or Barkington.

"And now?" Hentie repeated.

I faced her.

She sat with Barkington in her lap. He was half asleep, but dressed in a cute gray waist coat that matched Hentie's PJ set. Her hair was down out of its floppy bun for once. She looked utterly exhausted, like the past few days had worn on her.

I'd been so busy trying to figure this out, I'd almost forgotten how much she had to be struggling. First, she'd lost Franklin, and then she'd discovered he'd been having an affair with a younger and much more annoying woman.

"I'm sorry, Hentie," I said.

"Ag, sorry for what? You haven't done anything wrong." Hentie shifted Barkington in her lap and he whined, complaining at the interruption. His eyes drifted open and shut.

"I've been neglecting you," I said.

"Asseblief. It's not like I'm a toddler. I'm a grown up. And anyway, there's more important things to worry about than how I feel. What about that guy who broke into the house?"

"Guy? It could be a woman," I said.

And it couldn't be Emery or Dale. But did that mean it was Hadley or Mayor Barrera?

"Ja, it could definitely have been a woman," Hentie said, "but how do we figure it out?" She wriggled her nose from side-to-side. "Who would have wanted to kill Victoria."

"Most of the town, it seems. Dale had argued with her. Hadley certainly didn't like her. Emery isn't upset about her sister's death, and the mayor might have wanted to get rid of her because Victoria was competition."

"Competition?" Hentie asked.

"I have a theory that Victoria might have wanted to run for mayor in the upcoming election," I said. "I have to talk to Emery and find out if it's true, and I planned on doing it this evening until all of this happened."

Hentie yawned, pressing a hand over her mouth. "Sjoe, I'm tired. This has been too exciting."

"Hentie," I said. "Do you think you can figure out when Franklin bought the house and who he bought it from?" I was too wired to be tired. The attack, Smulder's decision to try to leave, and it felt like I was close. Closer than ever. If I could just make these puzzle pieces fit together, I'd have the answer.

"Ja, I think so," she said. "I would have to talk to the solicitor. I'm sorry I didn't ask before, I just—I have been distracted."

"This is *not* your fault. None of it is." And then I turned toward the window again, assessing the moonlit yard.

It wasn't memories that threatened to drift to the

surface this time, but emotions. The feelings of betrayal and sadness, of something bordering on heartbreak.

Brian wants to leave. He can't stand being around you. You've driven him away.

And then a memory did flash into view. Mickey, my late boyfriend, lying on the floor, gone from this world. Gone forever. He'd dropped right in front of me.

Enough.

Barkington let out a grumpy bark as Hentie rose from my armchair.

"I'm going to try to get some sleep," she said. "We'll see if I can manage. Isn't that right, Blaffies?"

Another whine.

I went over and gave Bark a kiss goodnight on his fluffy head. "See you in the morning," I said to Hentie. "Be safe."

"I'm going to lock my door and my windows, don't worry."

"Hentie," I called.

She looked back at me, her gray eyebrows lifting. "Ja?"

"Did you unlock the basement door?" I asked. "I'm sure that I locked it the last time I used it."

"I didn't unlock it," she replied. "You know what I'm like, April. I like to lock and double-lock everything." She had that habit from living in South Africa. "I checked it was locked before I started making aandete. Dinner."

"Thanks," I said.

She left me to my thoughts.

And my plans.

I had to rule these suspects out. Emery was out. Dale wasn't the right size.

But what about Mayor Barrera? I'd thought she was invested in keeping the town safe, and that was her only motive for delaying the murder investigation, but now I knew better.

I sat down on the edge of my bed, scanning my room, my gaze coming to a rest on my fanny pack, which I'd placed on the bedside table beside me. I couldn't go running around, vaulting fences, and invading people's personal space with a broken wrist. Well, I could, but I'd be way less efficient.

Instead, I grabbed my phone from my pocket and opened a search browser.

I searched up Mayor Barrera's office number, then started snooping around. Her social media profiles. Her website.

Her personal mobile number was listed on her website.

I copied it with a swipe of my fingers. A quick scan of her social media profiles told me nothing new. She loved Tickle, she was a passionate politician, and she had followed and liked *Travel Texas,* the online magazine that published the list of tourist destinations in Texas.

Nothing that I could use to prove she had been a part of this.

The only leads I had were her insistence that Remington refuse to investigate and her mention of having been near the mansion on the night of the murder. But why would she have admitted that?

Victoria's death had been mocking. Someone had wanted to prove that she wasn't as clean and upstanding as everyone had assumed. The lipstick crosses that looked like prohibition era proof markings, and the method of death suggested that.

I navigated to a secret folder on my phone and opened the suite of apps I kept for occasions like these.

One was a hacking app I had designed myself.

Another was an app I was currently testing. A method of hacking into people's phones using their number alone.

I opened the app and pasted Mayor Barrera's number into it, then grabbed my earphones from the fanny pack. I hit the button on the app to hack into the phone, then inserted my earphones and lay down on my bed, fully clothed, to wait.

Barrera wouldn't be on her phone constantly, but when she did make a call I should, theoretically, be able to hear it.

I'd done a little testing with the app and it had been buggy. I'd have to hope that this time would be the exception, or that I'd at least get to hear *something* of use. I was desperate. Desperate enough to use improperly tested software so I could get a lead.

My eyes drifted shut as I waited for a call to pop through.

&

"—ANY IDEA WHAT TIME IT IS?" A WOMAN'S voice shocked me awake.

Sunlight streamed through my window, and I blinked.

"Sorry, Mayor, but I thought you'd want to hear about this first thing, it being about Victoria Dawson and all." Sheriff Remington's drawl was clear in my earphones.

I'd fallen asleep with them in, and thank goodness for that. I lifted my phone and checked the time. It was past seven in the morning and my phone battery was on ten percent. I got out of bed and put the phone on charge.

"I thought I told you to drop this, Colton," Barrera said. "Why are you disobeying a direct order?"

"All due respect, Mayor, but you aren't my boss. You can't tell me what to do." Remington's voice trembled. Was he afraid of her? "I brought Emery Dawson in for questioning."

"What?" Barrera snapped it out.

I moved through to the tiny en suite bathroom and

splashed water on my face as I listened to them talk. I braced myself on the sink, staring at my reflection. Tired eyes, dark circles, my short dark hair in disarray.

"I released her this morning, but I brought her in for questioning, and she had some interesting things to say."

"Colton. I don't care what—"

The call cut out, and I muttered under my breath.

"—Victoria was the one who did it. And that you knew."

"And so what if I did know? It was a float," Barrera replied. "Victoria had a problem with Hadley."

"But don't you see how that looks?" Remington asked. "You being near the house on the night of the murder..."

"I only went to the darn mansion to warn her," Barrera said, waspishly. "Not that it's anyone's business, but Victoria had crossed the line, and I wanted to make sure she didn't do it again."

A silence.

I clasped the edge of the sink.

"This is ridiculous," Barrera said. "You can't seriously think I had anything to do with this."

"Where were you yesterday after the town meeting?"

"I was on my way home," she said. "You know that."

"I might need to see your phone records," he replied.

"Colton! What is your darn problem?"

"My problem is that everyone in this town has gone

stir crazy over the holidays. And you're more than happy to let it happen so you can protect your position as mayor, but what you don't realize is that the longer we let this go, the worse it will get. You aren't the only one Emery Dawson implicated last night."

Oh?

Mayor Barrera hesitated.

"Dale Dunnels," he said. "Apparently, he's been threatening Emery about her inheritance and about Victoria's will."

"Why would I care if—?"

"Because it's a symptom of the sickness in this town. Everything you've been trying to do, keep the peace, clean the place up, make it wholesome, it's back fired. There's been a murder, there's extortion, home invasions, theft. We can't keep lying to people. The public has a right to know."

"Remington. I'm done with this conversation. The only thing the people of Tickle need to know is—"

The call cut out, and I checked the app.

An error had popped up on the screen. I cleared it and tried to reconnect, but the voices of Barrera and the sheriff didn't return.

"Darn." I disconnected my earbuds.

Red lines spread across the corkboard in my mind, connecting from Dale seated in front of the row of skulls to that image of Dale confronting Emery underneath the tree. Was that it? He wanted something from her? Money? But why?

The main fuzzy image, the one I was sure would reveal the truth had cleared even more. I almost recognized the background, but it was too blurry.

Barrera and Dunnels. Emery and Hadley. My main suspects.

Hadley didn't have an alibi for the night of the murder or the time of the home invasion. Neither did Dale or Barrera. The only person who was clear was Emery.

And she seemed to know a lot more than she'd initially told me.

I brushed my teeth and freshened up, my mind on the next steps and that deadline.

Two days.

Twenty-Seven

Hentie and Bark had opted for breakfast in the guesthouse's quaint dining room, with its view of the trees and the neatly kept garden out front. I bid them good morning, then grabbed a croissant to go and headed out the door with the promise to return later.

I didn't want Hentie and Bark coming along with me this time.

My fanny pack of spy tools was strapped into place, and I had to make this quick and dirty if necessary. Usually, I wouldn't resort to these measures, but Grant wanted me out of town, and I planned on making that happen fast.

Smulder didn't stop me on my way out. I hadn't seen him since last night.

I got into the I Scream for Ice Cream truck and drove

off, my hands clasping the steering wheel so hard that my knuckles whitened.

It was a struggle to keep the images on the corkboard at bay after what I'd heard this morning.

Barrera at the mansion. Dale threatening the Dawson family. And Emery being questioned about Victoria's death.

It couldn't be Emery. It couldn't be. Unless she'd found a way to be in two places at once.

I parked in front of the Dawson house and got out. A Honda was parked near the front steps, and I frowned. Wasn't this Dale's car? Was he here to threaten Emery again?

I jogged up the front steps and knocked on the front door.

It drifted inward.

"—call the cops," Emery said.

"You've already done that," Dale replied. "Do you think I'm afraid of them? I don't care if they come out here looking for me. I haven't done anything wrong."

"Threatening people is the wrong thing to do." Emery's voice was quiet, as always, like she was afraid to use it.

"It amazes me that you've found your voice," Dale snapped. "You wouldn't say a word when I tried to talk to before."

"Leave my house. Now."

"This isn't your house," Dale said. "It's mine."

"You're delusional."

I stalked down the hall, my steps muffled through practice and by the runner carpet that lay across polished wooden boards. This mansion was as stately as Hentie's, and even creepier than I'd anticipated, if that was possible.

I stopped outside the entry to the living room on my right, listening hard.

"—without proof."

"Every time I've tried to talk to you about the proof I have, you've ignored me," Dale said. "I've spent my life working up to this moment. Researching. Poring over historical documents. I'm not going to let this slide."

"I can't help you."

"I don't care if you can't help me," he said. "You're going to give me what I'm owed regardless."

"This is dumb," Emery said. "We're going in circles. I am not giving you my inheritance. Victoria told me about you, Dunnels. How you're a scammer and a cheat. My father *never* had an affair with a woman out of state, so you can take your vicious lies and leave my house." And then a slap rang out.

Uh oh.

I wasn't about to stand by and let violence ensue on

my watch. I stepped around the corner and found Emery standing, palm raised, and Dale clutching his left cheek.

"You'll pay for that," he growled.

"Stop it," I said.

Both of them jerked on the spot. Emery gasped, and Dale let out a girlish shriek, then spun to face me.

"What the—? What are *you* doing here?"

"I came to see Emery," I said. "I knocked. Nobody answered."

"So, that means you just walk right in?" Dale countered.

"I heard raised voices. Seems I was right. You two good?" I directed that at Emery.

She sniffed and gave the barest hint of a nod. "Dale was just leaving."

"I am *not* leaving. And I'm done playing nice. Your family owes me money. You owe me my life back," Dale said.

"What do you mean?" I asked, though I had a hunch what he was talking about.

Dale cracked his fingers, pulling on them nervously. "I wasn't going to tell anyone about this, but I—"

Emery snorted. "You weren't going to tell anyone?" She lowered herself into a leather armchair and reached for a pack of cigarettes on the table. She removed one and lit it with a shaking hand. "You've been torturing us for months now. Years. Ever since you came to town and started taunting Victoria about our past and trying to—" She broke off and grimaced at the cigarette then put it out in a silver ashtray on the table.

The cigarette butt was yellow.

An image flashed in my eyes—a long white cigarette butt on the path in front of the Dawson house, freshly dropped by Victoria.

"You two have made it impossible for me to prove my case," he said. "What did you expect me to do? Sit back and let it happen?"

"What case?" I asked.

"I'm the rightful heir to this house," Dale said.

His announcement was met with a sigh and an eye roll from Emery. "He's been making claims like this for months now. Blackmailing my sister and trying to get her to give him money. He's a scammer."

"I am not. Your father, Dalton Dawson, is the same as my father."

A lot of "D" names floating around in these parts.

"We asked you to prove it, and you haven't."

"Oh, but I have," Dale said. "Just because you're too stupid to understand the facts doesn't mean I haven't proved it. Her father had an affair with my mother, thirty years ago. And here I am. He didn't take responsibility for me. He rejected my mother at every turn. I've spent my life working as a historian to uncover the truth about the Dawson family and about my true heritage."

"Except he's not a historian. He's a fraud."

"I am *not* a fraud."

"You didn't study at any acclaimed university or institution," Emery said, ticking things off on her fingers from where she sat on the sofa. "You haven't studied history. You haven't—"

"You don't have to study history to be a historian," Dale said, puffing out his chest. "I've found out the truth."

"If you have all this evidence," Emery said. "Why don't you just go to a lawyer." She'd really come into herself since her sister had passed on. Interesting.

I took a snapshot of her on the sofa, beside the cigarettes that weren't hers. Dale's? No. Surely not.

"Lawyer's cost money," Dale said.

"Yeah, but you could sue me for the money to pay for the lawyer, assuming you're correct about this," Emery said, cocking her head to the side and arching her eyebrows. "But you don't have a case. Do you? Otherwise you'd already have done that."

Dale huffed and puffed.

"All you're trying to do is extort me," Emery said. "And it ends today."

"I am not extorting anyone. I'm going to get what belongs to me," Dale said. "I am your brother, whether you like it or not, and I'm not going to spend the rest of my life suffering in poverty while you sit in a house that shouldn't belong solely to you. Trash!"

Emery inhaled then released the breath on a sharp smile. "If you don't want to live in poverty, then why don't you get a *real* job. Mr. Historian."

Dale took a step toward her, and I cast out a hand.

"Don't," I said.

"I didn't invite you in here," Emery said. "You barged into my house unannounced. You're lucky I don't call the cops on you right now."

"You won't," Dale hissed. "You wouldn't dare."

And, strangely, Emery recoiled at his words. Like what he'd said was true.

Dale had been trying to extort Victoria and now Emery, but he was too large to have been the attacker who'd burst into Hentie's mansion. And Emery had been in custody at the time, so it couldn't be her either.

This felt like a waste of time.

Except Emery reached for those cigarettes then shook her head and pulled a face. They definitely weren't hers. And they looked almost identical to the cigarette that had been at the crime scene.

Emery said something, but I wasn't listening. I was focused on her lips moving. Red lipstick. But it would be impossible to match her lipstick to the markings on Victoria's cheeks. And since when did Emery wear lipstick?

"—at least a thousand dollars," Dale said.

Emery laughed loudly. An anomaly for her. "You're out of your mind. You want me to pay you to leave? And what if I say no?"

"Then I'll make you pay with—"

"I wouldn't finish that sentence if I were you." Hadley McCulloch strode into the living room, her shocking red hair tied into a ponytail that accentuated her high cheekbones. "Is this guy bothering you again, Emery?"

Twenty-Eight

Hadley cast me a quick glance and a smile. "Did you decide to host a party without me, Em?" Hadley laughed at her own joke. "Seriously, what's everyone doing here? This is kooky beans."

"Sorry, Hadley," Emery said, with a bob of her head, her voice quieting. "Dale came in without my permission, and so did April. But I think that was because she wanted to protect me."

"I heard shouting," I added in, for context.

Hadley took up a spot in front of Dale, staring down at him through narrowed sparkling green eyes. Dale's fluffy hair seemed to stick out in response, like fur rising on a cat's back. Except, that wasn't possible and it was all perspective. I was finding meaning in these actions, because my brain was working on the problem.

"I thought I told you to leave her alone, Dunnels," Hadley said. "Nobody messes with my friends."

"Do you think you scare me?" Dale's tone trembled.

"Judging by the layer of sweat on your forehead, I'm going to go with yes, yes I do think I scare you. I can smell your fear from here." Hadley was full of sass. I would've admired her if not for the truth that was unfolding in my mind.

"I'm not scared of *you*," Dale said. "You're just... You and your friend are bullies. Just because you're well-connected, doesn't make you the boss of this town."

"You need to leave," Emery chimed in. She was calmer now that Hadley was here, perhaps because she felt safer?

Dale backed away from Hadley's stare moving toward the archway that led into the living room.

Hadley stared him down as he moved. "That's right, buddy. Back it on up."

"I know." The words dropped from Dale's lips.

Hadley stiffened, her eyes widening then narrowing again in a flash. "What?"

"I know. I know about what you've done."

Emery had gone still in her seat, her hands grasping the legs of her jeans.

"And what is it that you think I've done, Dale?" Hadley asked.

"I heard the rumors. I know things," he said.

"That's very nice, buddy," Hadley replied, her shoulders lowering a little as she gave Emery a smile. The other woman struggled to return this. "Get a load of this guy. Thinks he's Nostradamus or something."

"I know you were having an affair with a married man," Dale said.

Emery relaxed. Hadley burst out laughing. "Kooky beans. I'm telling you. Absolutely kooky beans." She twirled her finger next to her head.

"I saw you," Dale said. "Visiting him. I saw—"

"All right, now that's enough." Hadley strode toward him. "You'd better get out of here before I make you. Got it? Shut your mouth and get out. I've had enough of these garbage rumors in this town."

Dale gnawed on his bottom lip, but backed away. Finally, he turned on his heel and fled from the room. A moment later, a door slammed shut.

Hadley grimaced. "Sorry about that," she said, taking a seat on a reclining chair in the living room. "He's a *special* individual. Like, he really thinks he can go around extorting people."

"I hope the cops deal with him," I said, shaking my head, even as I put the pieces together.

"I don't know if they will," Emery replied. "I've asked them multiple times to get him to stop harassing me, and they won't do anything about it. They say there's no proof."

"What about Victoria?" I asked, assessing their body language. Another stiffening. A quick glance from Hadley toward Emery. "Did she ever report him?"

"Oh yeah," Emery said, with a small smile. "She thought he was the person who broke in and stole—"

Hadley cleared her throat. "These are mine, right?" She grabbed the pack of cigarettes from the table.

"Yeah." Emery laughed nervously. "I tried to smoke one earlier and I nearly died. I don't know how you stand those things, Hads. They're super strong."

"Look," I said, and both women lifted their heads. I was keenly aware that I had a broken wrist and that made me less effective in a fight. "I'm sorry for coming in here unannounced. I came by to check on you, Emery. I heard a rumor that you got arrested, and I thought there was no way that was true. You've always been so kind."

"Aw, you're sweet," Emery said. "It was Remington making a big deal out of nothing. Anyway, I'm fine. But you look hurt. What happened to your—?"

"It's a good thing you got here when you did," Hadley said, lighting up her cigarette. "Who knows what he would have tried if you hadn't arrived." She paused, a smirk pulling at the corners of her lips. "Nice fanny pack by the way."

"Yeah." Emery checked her pockets for her pack of cigarettes and frowned when she couldn't find them. "He was starting to get heated."

"I'm sorry you're going through that," I said, then checked my watch and clicked my tongue. "All right, well, you're good, so I guess I don't have to be worried. I'd better get back to the house. Hentie's waiting on me. We're thinking of making cookies today." It was a blatant lie. "I'll drop by with some for you later."

"That would be amazing," Emery said. "Thanks for caring, April. You're a gem."

"You're going to make me blush." I grinned back at her, then turned to Hadley. "I don't know if I ever got the chance to thank you for warning me about Victoria. It's terrible that she's gone, but if you hadn't told me, I wouldn't have attended that meeting. The thought of our truck getting in trouble doesn't sit right with me."

"Of course." Hadley waved the cigarette around, tapping ash off the end into the ash tray. "Anything to keep the people of this town happy."

I bid them farewell then strolled up the hall at a leisurely pace. I exited and immediately broke into a trot. I got into the truck, started the engine and drove down the long road that led away from the house. Once I was out of sight, I parked and texted Hentie.

> Can you meet me back at the house, fast?

I waited impatiently for a response. This had nothing to do with making cookies.

My phone blipped a moment later.

> Ja. Why, what's wrong?

> I need to talk to you about something important. In person.

> Okay. I can be there in like fifteen minutes.

See you soon.

I navigated out of my text message thread with Hentie and created a new one with Smulder. I was in the habit of deleting my messages whenever I could.

> We're leaving today.

Three dots appeared at the bottom of the screen, then disappeared again.

"Come on," I muttered, starting up the engine of the ice cream truck.

Finally, Smulder's response came through.

"Wow. Nice. Okay," I said, and placed my phone on the seat beside me. Finally, I started off down the road. Five minutes later, I pulled up outside Hentie's mansion. It was quiet, and the morning was cool and overcast.

I got out of the truck and headed inside, locking the door behind me. I checked the basement door and found it unlocked. My suspicions grew. Mental images on the corkboard swam into focus and out of it. I locked the basement door and moved a heavy table in front of it, then went upstairs to my bedroom.

I mimicked what Smulder had done earlier in the week and tore my closest open. I grabbed my suitcase and walked it over to the bed, then started packing.

Time flew by, and the images rose and fell. The blurry image was almost completely clear.

My stomach turned and sweat broke out on my brow.

It was so obvious.

It was so painfully obvious, now. I needed that final piece of evidence, and then we were good to go. I could end this and move on from this town.

A door shut downstairs, and Barkington's greeting barks rang out. "April?" Hentie called. "April, are you home?"

"I'm in my room!" I called back.

Hentie's steps came up the stairs, and Barkington yapped excitedly from my doorway.

"Hey, Bark," I said.

"Oh, jinne. What's going on?" Hentie asked. "Are we leaving?"

I liked that she'd said "we." I had a friend. A real, true friend, which was something I had never had growing up. Being friends with anyone had been difficult thanks to my mother.

"We're leaving," I said. "Soon. I can't tell you why, but it's important."

Barkington whined his concern.

"Okay," Hentie said, wriggling her nose. "But what about the murder? The police aren't sommer going to let me leave."

"Sommer?"

"Simply."

"Right. That's the *other* thing I wanted to talk to you about," I said, and sat down on the wooden chest at the end of my bed.

"DID YOU FIND OUT WHO OWNED THIS HOUSE before Franklin bought it?" I asked.

"Actually, yes," Hentie said, setting Barkington down. He pittered over to me and licked my ankles. I lifted him up and sat him in my lap, petting him as my friend filled me in. "The solicitor said that it was a quick sale, about three years ago, which was about six months before we moved here."

"Who did he buy it from?" This had been a McCulloch house, but had Hadley lived in it? That was the important part. Emery had told me she hadn't, but I couldn't trust her word.

"Beau McCulloch," Hentie said. "I did research on who this guy was after I found out, and it turns out that he was Hadley's father. He passed away shortly after the sale of the house and is buried in the local cemetery."

"So this place was, indeed, Hadley's house," I said.

"Ja. That's what it seems like."

"Give me a second." I stopped petting Bark and raised my good hand. I shut my eyes, ticking my fingers as I rifled through the information.

Flashes of images appeared in the darkness.

Hadley lighting up a cigarette that matched the one found at the scene.

Emery with her painting of the key. Emery's claim that she'd thrown her copy of the key out. The way she'd gone from barely speaking to talking and laughing loudly. Her attitude around Hadley, an image of their awkward behavior in the living room.

And the affair.

An affair between Franklin and the victim, Victoria.

And then, another claimed affair by Dale. He hadn't got to tell me who Hadley was having an affair with, but if it was Franklin, then that gave her a motive. Both of them had a motive. And while Emery had an alibi for yesterday's home invasion, Hadley did not.

The picture on my corkboard cleared in a flash.

In it, Hadley leaned against the wall in the town hall, glaring at Victoria. She clasped an object in her right hand, a metal item that flashed in the fluorescent lights. I pinched my fingers together and released them, zooming in on the image.

Three circles linked together, ending in a shaft that was hidden beneath Hadley's fingers.

A key. And one that looked identical to the picture Emery had been painting.

Hadley's house.

She would have known about that secret room. And if we'd never found it, Victoria would have been declared missing rather than dead. Even so, it had been declared an accident.

Now, how was I going to prove this to the police?

It wasn't like I could trot out my corkboard pictures in front of them and show them what I'd discovered.

I was certain that Emery and Hadley had been working together to get rid of Victoria.

The evidence I needed?

Proof that Hadley or Emery had pure ethanol. The cigarettes. The keys. And then, of course, I'd have to get Dale to tell me what he knew about Hadley's affair.

My eyes snapped open.

"If I wanted to hide evidence, I wouldn't hide it in my house," I said.

Hentie frowned. Barkington yapped.

"No," I said. "I wouldn't do that. I'd hide it where

nobody would check. And what better place to hide something, than in a place that was used to hide illegal items before?"

"The tunnels?" Hentie asked.

"The tunnels. Hentie," I said. "Can you do me a favor and call Oliver? I would love it if he came home and started packing his stuff too. We're going to leave very soon. Within the next few hours."

"Ag, okay," Hentie replied. "But I haven't packed anything yet."

"Pack everything you want to take with you," I said. "I promise, I wouldn't ask you to leave this house if—"

Hentie laughed. "April, I've wanted to leave this place ever since you found Victoria's body. And since the solicitor told me about Franklin's affair. I can't... I don't want to deal with this stuff. I just want to sell this house and move on with my life, because I feel like—" She broke off.

"Like you've been betrayed," I said.

"Ja."

I gave a firm nod then got up and gave Barkington to her. "I've got to do a few things before we leave."

"Lekker," Hentie said. "I'll phone Oliver and go pack quickly."

And then she left the room, which was exactly what I needed. I didn't want her overhearing the conversation I was about to have. I lifted my phone off the wooden chest and searched up Dale's number online.

"This is Dale Dunnels," he answered, "historian specializing in all things Texas and prohibition. If you're calling for an interview, please email me instead, as I am busy with important research that shouldn't be interrupted unless it's an emergency." He sounded like an answering machine.

"Hi Dale," I said. "It's April Waters. Who was Hadley having an affair with?"

He gulped.

"You can tell me," I said. "I won't tell a soul."

"I'm afraid she'll do something if I tell you." I could almost hear Dale sweating through the phone.

"You didn't seem very afraid this morning," I said. "You stood up to her."

"That was because there were people around. She's dangerous." Dale hesitated. "If you swear not to tell a soul, I can fill you in."

"I think it's your duty to reveal these things," I said, playing into his ego. "You're the truth teller in Tickle. You're the one that exposed the Dawson family's history."

"You're right," Dale said, and then his voice strengthened. "Of course, you're right. Dangerous or not, nobody bullies a Dunnels."

"I thought you were a Dawson."

"Yeah, that too!" The sound of a cigarette being lit punctuated the quiet. "She was having an affair with Franklin Cooper. It was a badly kept secret within her family. She got disowned by her father because of it."

"Beau?"

"That's the one," he said. "He was unimpressed with the way she was behaving."

"So this dated back how far? This affair?"

"Years," Dale said.

Motive. I had a motive for Hadley and for Emery, as well. Interesting that Franklin hadn't left anything to Hadley in his will, since he'd been having an affair with her too. *Poor Hentie.*

"Do you have any proof?" I asked.

"Sure do," Dale said, barely skipping a beat. "I've got pictures."

Did I want to know why Dunnels had been taking pictures of Hadley? Then again, it fit with his M.O. for the Dawsons. He wanted to blackmail them into giving him what he wanted. And while that was disgusting and illegal, it helped my case.

"Do you think you can forward them to me? Or put them in an online folder or something?"

"What's in it for me?" I could picture Dale rubbing his hands together, greedily.

I frowned. *Oh, Dale. You sweet summer child.* "I guess,

what's in it for you is that I don't go to the police and give them the recording of this phone call."

"You can't do that!"

"Texas is a one-party consent state, Dale." Which wasn't how this worked, but he didn't need to know that. I had to scare him like he'd scared and threatened Emery.

Dale babbled for a second.

"The police would be interested to hear that you've been blackmailing people in Tickle," I said.

"They already know that. Emery told them."

"Yeah, but Emery didn't have any proof. I do," I said.

Dale choked on a breath, then said, "Fine. I'll send you the pictures. But don't tell anyone where you got them from."

"Scout's honor." Likely, I wouldn't have to tell the cops anything.

I hung up the call and waited for the message to come through with the attached images. Once it had, I transferred those images to my laptop and then onto a thumb drive.

I placed the drive in my fanny pack, put a glove on my good hand, then started for the door. Doing everything one-handed was challenging, but doable, and I wasn't about to stop now on account of a busted wrist. I exited into the hall, listening as Hentie talked to Smulder on the phone.

I'd messaged Smulder, but hearing it from her would hopefully spur him on to get here and start packing.

I started down the stairs, my focus on the basement door and the task ahead.

Proving that Hadley McCulloch had killed Victoria, without a shadow of a doubt.

Thirty

I HELD MY FLASHLIGHT ALOFT AS I NAVIGATED the tunnels underneath the mansion, blocking out errant thoughts. I focused on my breath and the present moment, heightening my awareness.

There was silence down here, a damp tension that seeped through the bricks and set the hair on the back of my neck standing on end.

The gate that separated the two tunnels was unlocked, as if the attacker had forgotten to lock it or refused to do so. Perhaps, they'd been too afraid to return to these tunnels after their escape. With the cops interested in what had happened—albeit vaguely thanks to Remington's hesitation—I didn't blame them.

Hadley. It's Hadley.

I had spent so long unsure of who had done this that I

was in the habit of referring to the attacker as an anonymous person.

But it was her. Hadley, who had killed Victoria as an act of revenge and likely with Emery's help.

I found the off-shoot tunnel where I'd broken my wrist and lifted the flashlight. The beam washed the crumbling bricks a pale red, and I studied them, intently. Unlike the entrance to the secret room in the mansion, there was no button to press to open that wall.

And that made sense. Hadley had disappeared quickly when she'd run into this tunnel ahead of me.

I stepped back and tapped on the brick flooring.

Tap. Tap. Nothing. *Tap. Tap.* Come on, where had she gone to? There had to be a secret room here. The evidence pointed toward it. *Tap. Tap. Thonk.*

Bingo.

I patted the brick in question with the heel of my trainer. *Thonk, thonk.* And then I pressed down hard. *Click.*

A section of the flooring popped up and out.

I opened it and found a tunnel beneath, similar to the entry point behind the oak tree at the Dawson mansion.

The tunnel below was lit with cold light, so I pocketed my phone and descended, pausing to shut the entrance behind me, so that it would appear as if no one had come this way.

I used my good arm to climb down the ladder then hopped into the tunnel below.

The tunnel was actually a room, lit by a small fluorescent lamp in the corner. Two chairs had been shoved into one corner. Beside them, on the floor, were several bottles of pure ethanol. On an overturned crate, sat a key—three circles, a shaft decorated in floral patterns.

There was no other exit to the room.

Hadley must've hid here and waited until the coast was clear before leaving again.

Everything was down here. The evidence, the murder weapon, and now, the thumb drive of pictures. I removed it from my fanny pack and placed it beside the key.

I got my phone out and scrolled through my contacts until I found Hadley's number. Then, I snapped a picture of the murder weapon and sent it to her, without any further details. That *should* be enough.

Afterward, I immediately texted Hentie.

Please take Bark and go meet up with Smulder. Stay with him.

I'm already with him. We're loading our stuff into the truck.

Good. Stay up there, okay? Once this is done, we're leaving.

Okay, lekker.

This was short notice, but we had to be out now.

I unzipped my fanny pack and removed a monocle. I placed it over my right eye then brought out my favorite silver mallet. Finally, I switched off the fluorescent light in the corner and plunged the small hiding space into darkness.

Not long now.

I tapped the side of the monocle and the room was washed in green light for me. State of the art night vision for when I couldn't put in my night vision contact lenses. I walked over to the corner across from the ladder, and crouched down to wait.

Emery and Hadley had been at Emery's house. It wouldn't take them long to get here, and I doubted that they would ignore the message. They weren't trained killers. Unlike me.

Ten minutes passed.

The trap door opened, and light flashed into the room.

"The light's off," Emery whispered.

"Shush. She might be in there," Hadley replied.

"There's no way. The light's off."

"Would you just get down there? You're the one who knew she was trying to figure this out, and you did nothing. You didn't even tell me. So, you go down there and find out what's going on."

Emery started down the ladder, the light from her phone illuminating the rungs. When she reached the bottom rung, I took a silent step forward and struck the side of her neck with my mallet. Emery toppled backward, her phone falling face down on the brick floor.

I caught her, with one arm, gritting my teeth at the burst of pain. That was going to hurt in the morning. I dragged Emery backward, depositing her in the corner. The vagus nerve was my favorite spot to hit—simply because it was less intrusive than other methods of incapacitating enemies.

Hadley didn't have the flashlight and she hadn't seen what had happened.

"Emery?" Hadley called out. "Emery, are you okay? Hello?"

I waited.

"What the heck? Emery. This is not funny." Hadley hesitated, then she came down the ladder. "Kooky beans," she muttered, as she reached the bottom rung.

Again, I stepped forward and struck Hadley on the neck. I caught her one-armed, releasing a breath at the increasing pain.

Should have just asked Smulder for help. But would he have helped me? Now wasn't the time to worry about that.

I laid the women down, side-by-side, then stowed my mallet and removed four cable ties from my fanny pack. I restrained their hands and feet, placed them on their sides, and checked their airways. Afterward, I removed my monocle and switched on the light in the corner.

The women didn't wake up.

I removed Hadley's phone from her pocket, and then used my hacking app to get into it. Finally, I deleted the text message and image I sent her, returned her phone to her pocket, and climbed up the ladder and out into the brick hall above.

Once I had reached Hentie's basement, I shut the trap door and the basement door thereafter, before lifting my phone and dialing 911.

"911, what is your emergency?"

"Hi," I said, affecting breathlessness. "Please, I need your help. I just saw two women disappear into the ground behind a tree. Please. There's a trap door, and they went in together, and I think something's wrong down there because I heard someone scream. You have to send help. Please!"

"Ma'am, please calm down. What is the exact address."

I sobbed and told her the address to the Dawson mansion. "It's right under an oak tree next to the lake. Please, you have to hurry."

"Stay on the line, ma'am. I've dispatched officers to your location."

"Oh my gosh, hurry!" And then I hung up and strolled out of the house and toward the ice cream truck where

Smulder already had the engine running and Hentie was sitting in the middle seat, waiting for me.

"Bark in his crate?" I asked.

"Ja."

"Let's blow this joint," I said, and patted the dashboard.

Smulder gave me a look, but didn't say anything as we took the road that circled the lake. In the distance, sirens interrupted the idyllic morning.

Thirty-One

That evening...

WE STOPPED AT A GAS STATION ON OUR WAY OUT of Texas to grab gas, snacks, and to stretch our legs. I'd insisted we keep driving for as long as possible before stopping, but we had taken breaks for Bark's sake several times during the afternoon.

Each time, I'd stood outside, watching that nothing happened. No cars following. No police or ambulances or anything of the like.

Hentie grabbed Barkington and cooed as she strolled toward the store. She hadn't asked questions, and she'd certainly sensed the mood in the truck. The longer we'd been on the road, the more tense Smulder had become.

"Grab me a bottle of water, please," I called after Hentie.

"I will," she said, and Barkington barked over her shoulder at me.

I waved at him, smiling.

"You want to explain what happened back there?" Smulder asked, cologne washing over me. He was standing too close.

I bit down on the inside of my cheek. I had a headache, my broken wrist was throbbing thanks to my "citizen's arrest", and I wasn't in the mood to hear it from him right now.

"Maybe another time, Oliver," I said. "Right now, I'm tired. I want to move onto another town, get through Christmas, and figure out what's next."

"What's next is maintaining your cover. What's next is—"

"Stop it," I said.

"What?" His brow furrowed. Darn him and his handsome frowns.

"Stop pretending that you care about me," I said. "Or about Hentie and Bark. Because I know you don't. You wanted to leave. And that's fine. But don't pretend that you didn't want to or that you care." I started walking toward the sliding glass doors that led into the store. Hentie was visible by the fridges, picking out sodas and water for us.

"I wanted to leave because I care," Smulder said.

I stopped, mid-stride, and a chill ran over me. Goosebumps. Goosebumps because... what was he saying?

"Delta," he murmured.

"Don't. You're not supposed to use my—"

"I'm in love with you."

My heart dropped then nearly took off. It felt as if it wanted to hammer its way out of my chest.

I turned toward him. "What did you say?"

"I'm falling... No, I *am* in love with you," Smulder said, walking over, closing the distance between us so rapidly, I lost my breath. "And it's not ideal."

"Oh, well—"

"Because the longer I'm with you, the more my feelings grow, and handling them is difficult for me. I can't be impartial when you're in trouble. I can't do my job properly. Me feeling this way about you puts you at risk. That's why I wanted to leave."

The cool night air surrounded us. The sounds of people talking at one of the cars filling up at a pump.

They had no idea who we were and never would. They were a couple. Two happy people who would continue on with their lives, maybe even get married, while we could *never* do that. It would be too risky.

Smulder stepped closer to me, his gaze dropping to my lips.

I swallowed.

"I don't want you to leave," I said. "But we can't."

"I know."

"It would ruin everything. It would—"

"Do you think I'm unaware of that?" Smulder asked. "That's exactly the reason I tried to leave."

It was tempting to kiss him. It was tempting to believe that we could make it work.

The tension expanded between us. The moment building to a crescendo. Brian leaned in, I rose onto tiptoe and—

Barkington barked behind us.

Smulder and I jumped apart.

"Oh, nee, Blaffies. You interrupted them. Don't stop on account of us," Hentie said, with a bright smile. "We're here for moral support." Barkington tapped his paws on Hentie's arm, tilting his floofy head to the side.

I laughed. Smulder chuckled, and the moment retreated. We'd have to discuss this later. I had a lot of thinking to do about how I'd handle this and what I wanted.

For now, we had a new town to find and explore, Christmas to enjoy, and our covers to maintain.

Surely, there would be no more murders.

Thanks for reading another of Hentie and Delta's adventures! The story continues in Chocolate Scoop Murder, out in January, 2025. Please sign up for my mailing list to be informed when it releases.

Visit www.rosiepointbooks.com to sign up and get two free books!

Craving More Cozy Mystery?

If you had fun with Delta Mission, you'll, love getting to know Charlie Mission and her butt-kicking grandmother, Georgina. You can read the first chapter of Charlie's story, *The Case of the Waffling Warrants*, below!

"Come in, Big G, come in." I spoke under my breath so that the flesh-colored microphone seated against my throat picked up my voice. "What is your status?"

My grandmother, Georgina—pet name Gamma, code name Big G—was out on a special operation. Reconnaissance at the newest guesthouse in our town, Gossip. The reason? First, she was an ex-spy, as was I, and second, the woman who'd opened the guesthouse was her mortal enemy and in direct competition with my grandmother's establishment, the Gossip Inn.

Who was this enemy, this bringer of potential financial doom?

A middle-aged woman with a penchant for wearing pashminas and annoying anyone who looked her way.

Jessie Belle-Blue.

It was rumored that even thinking the woman's name summoned a murder of crows.

"I repeat, Big G, what is your status?"

"I'm en route to the nest," my grandmother replied in my earpiece.

I let out a relieved sigh and exited my bedroom, heading downstairs to help with the breakfast service.

In the nine months since I had retired as a spy, life in Gossip had been normal. In the Gossip sense of the term. I'd expected that my job as a server, maid, and assistant would bring the usual level of "cat herding" inherent when working at the inn. Whether that involved tracking down runaway cats, literally, or providing a guest with a moist towelette after a fainting spell—tempers ran high in Gossip.

What was the reason for the craziness? Shoot, it had to be something in the water.

I took the main stairs two at a time and found my friend, the inn's chef, paging through her recipe book in the lime green kitchen. Lauren Harris wore her red hair in a French braid today, apron stretched over her pregnant belly.

"Morning," I said, "how are you today?"

"Madder than a fat cat on a diet." She slapped her recipe book closed and turned to me.

Uh oh. Looks like it's time for more cat herding.

"What's wrong?"

"My supplier is out of flour and sugar. Can you believe that?" Lauren huffed, smoothing her hands over her belly while the clock on the wall ticked away. Breakfast was in two hours and Lauren loved baking cupcakes as part of the meal.

"Do you have enough supplies to make cupcakes for this morning?"

"Yes. But just for today," Lauren replied. "The guests are going to love my new waffle cupcakes, and they'll be sore they can't get anymore after this batch is done. Why, I should go down there and wring Billy's neck for doing this to me. He knows I take an order of sugar and flour every week, and I get it at just above cost too. What's Georgina going to say?"

"Don't stress, Lauren," I said. "We'll figure it out."

"Right." She brightened a little. "I nearly forgot you're the one who "fixes" things around here." Lauren winked at me.

She was the only person in the entire town who knew that my grandmother and I had once been spies for the NSIB—the National Security Investigative Bureau. But the news that I had helped solve several murders had spread through town, and now, anybody and everybody with a problem would call me up asking for help. A lot of them offered me money. And I was selective about who I chose to help.

"I'll check it out for you if you'd like," I said. "The flour issue."

"Nah, that's OK. I'm sure Billy will get more stock this week. I'll lean on him until he squeals."

"Sounds like you've been picking up tips from Georgina."

Lauren giggled then returned to her super-secret recipe book—no one but she was allowed to touch it.

"What's on the menu this morning?" I asked.

Lauren was the boss in the kitchen—she told me what to do, and I followed her instructions precisely. If I did anything else, like trying to read the recipe for instance, the food would end up burned, missing ingredients or worse.

The only place I wasn't a "fixer" was in the Gossip Inn's kitchen.

"Bacon and eggs over easy, biscuits and gravy, waffle cupcakes and... oh, I can't make fresh baked bread, can I?"

"Tell her I'll bring some back with me from the

bakery." Gamma's voice startled me. Goodness, I'd forgotten about the earpiece—she could hear everything happening in the kitchen.

"I'll text Georgina and ask her to bring bread from the bakery."

"You're a lifesaver, Charlotte."

We set to work on the breakfast—it was 7:00 a.m. and we needed everything done within two hours—and fell into our easy rhythm of baking and cooking.

My grandmother entered the kitchen at around 8:30 a.m., dressed in a neat silk blouse and a pair of slacks rather than the black outfit she'd left in for her spy mission. Tall, willowy, and with neatly styled gray hair, Gamma had always reminded me of Helen Mirren playing the Queen.

"Good morning, ladies," she said, in her prim, British accent. "I bring bread and tidings."

"What did you find out?" I asked.

"No evidence of the supposed ghost tours," Gamma said.

We'd started hosting ghost tours at the inn recently, so of course Jessie Belle-Blue wanted to do the same. She was all about under-cutting us, but, thankfully, the Gossip Inn had a legacy and over 1,000 positive reviews on Trip-Advisor.

Breakfast time arrived, and the guests filled the quaint dining area with its glossy tables, creaking wooden floors, and egg yolk yellow walls. Chatter and laughter leaked through the swinging kitchen doors with their porthole windows.

"That's my cue," I said, dusting off my apron, and heading out into the dining room.

I picked up a pot of coffee from the sideboard where we kept the drinks station and started my rounds.

Most of the guests had gathered around a center table in the dining room, and bursts of laughter came from the group, accompanied by the occasional shout.

I elbowed my way past a couple of guests—nobody could accuse me of having great people skills—apologizing along the way until I reached the table. The last time something like this had happened, a murder had followed shortly afterward.

Not this time. No way.

"—the last thing she'd ever hear!" The woman seated at the table, drawing the attention, was vaguely familiar. She wore her dark hair in luscious curls, and tossed it as she spoke, looking down her upturned nose at the people around the table.

"What happened then, Mandy?" Another woman asked, her hands clasped together in front of her stomach.

Mandy? Wait a second, isn't this Mandy Gilmore?

Gamma had mentioned her once before—Mandy was

a massive gossip in town. Why wasn't she staying at her house?

"What happened? Well, she ran off with her tail between her legs, of course. She'll soon learn not to cross me. Heaven knows, I always repay my debts."

"What, like a Lannister from *Game of Thrones*?" That had come from a taller woman with ginger curls.

"Shut up, Opal," Mandy replied. "You have no idea what we're talking about, and even if you did, you wouldn't have the intelligence to comprehend it."

The crowd let out various 'oofs' in response to that. The woman next to me clapped her hand over her mouth.

"You're all talk, Gilmore." Opal lifted a hand and yammered it at the other woman. "You act like you're a threat, but we know the truth around here."

"The truth?" Mandy leaned in, pressing her hands flat onto the tabletop, the crystal vase in the center rattling. "And what's that, Opal, darling? I'd love to hear it."

"That you're a failure. You sold your house, left Gossip with your head in the clouds, told everyone you were going to become a successful businesswoman, and now you're back. Back to scrape together the pieces of the life you have left."

"Witch!" Mandy scraped her chair back.

"All right, all right," I said, setting down the coffee pot

on the table. "That's enough, ladies. Everyone head back to their tables before things get out of hand."

Both Opal and Mandy stared daggers at me.

I flashed them both smiles. "We wouldn't want to ruin breakfast, would we? Lauren's prepared waffle cupcakes."

That distracted them. "Waffle cupcakes?" Opal's brow wrinkled. "How's that going to work?"

"Let's talk about it at your table." I grabbed my coffee pot and walked her away from Mandy. The crowd slowly dispersed, people muttering regret at having missed out on a show. The Gossip Inn was popular for its constant conflict.

If the rumors didn't start here then they weren't worth repeating. That was the mantra, anyway.

I seated Opal at her table, and she pursed her lips at me. "You shouldn't have interrupted. That woman needs a piece of my mind."

"We prefer peace of mind at the inn." I put up another of my best smiles.

Compared to what I'd been through in the past—hiding out from my rogue spy ex-husband and eventually helping put him behind bars when he found me—dealing with the guests was a cakewalk.

"What brings you to Gossip, Opal?" I asked.

"I live here," she replied, waspishly. "I'm staying here while they're fumigating my house. Roaches."

"Ah." I struggled not to grimace. Thankfully, my cell phone buzzed in the front pocket of my apron and distracted me. "Coffee?"

"I don't take caffeine." And she said it like I'd offered her an illegal substance too.

"Call me if you need anything." I hurried off before she could make good on that promise, bringing my phone out of my pocket.

I left the coffee pot on the sideboard, moving into the Gossip Inn's spacious foyer, the chandelier overhead off, but catching light in glimmers. The tables lining the hall were filled with trinkets from the days when the inn had been a museum—an eclectic collection of bits and bobs.

"This is Charlotte Smith," I answered the call—I would never get to use my true last name, Mission, again, but it was safer this way.

"Hello, Charlotte." A soft, rasping voice. "I've been trying to get through to you. I'm desperate."

"Who is this?"

"My name is Tina Rogers, and I need your help."

"My help."

"Yes," she said. "I understand that you have a certain set of skills. That you fix people's problems?"

"I do. But it depends on the problem and the price." I didn't have a set fee for helping people, but if it drew me away from the inn for long, I had to charge. I was technically a consultant now. Sort of like a P.I. without the fedora and coffee-stained shirt.

"My mother will handle your fee," Tina said. "I've asked her to text you about it, but I... I don't have long to talk. They're going to pull me off the phone soon."

"Who?"

"The police," she replied. "I'm calling you from the holding cell at the Gossip Police Station. I've been arrested on false charges, and I need you to help me prove my innocence."

"Miss Rogers, it's probably a better idea to invest in a lawyer." But I was tempted. It had been a long time since I'd felt useful.

"No! I'm not going to a lawyer. I'm going to make these idiots pay for ever having arrested me."

I took a breath. "OK. Before I accept your... case, I'll need to know what happened. You'll need to tell me every-thing." I glanced through the open doorway that led into the dining room. No one looked unhappy about the lack of service yet.

"I can't tell you everything now. I don't have much time."

"So give me the *CliffsNotes*."

"I was arrested for breaking into and vandalizing Josie Carlson's bakery, The Little Cake Shop. Apparently, they found my glove there—it was specially embroidered, you see—but it's not mine because—" The line went dead.

"Hello? Miss Rogers?" I pulled the cellphone away from my ear and frowned at the screen. "Darn."

My interest was piqued. A mystery case about a break-in that involved the local bakery? Which just so happened to be run by one of my least favorite people in Gossip?

And when I'd just started getting bored with the push and pull of everyday life at the inn?

Count me in.

Want to read more? You can grab **the first book** in *the Gossip Cozy Mystery series* on all major retailers.

Happy reading, friend!

Sign up to my mailing list and receive updates on future releases, as well as **FREE** copies of *The Hawaiian Burger Murder* and *The Fully Loaded Burger Murder*.

They are short cozy mystery featuring characters from *the Burger Bar Mystery series*.

Head to my website to sign up:
www.rosiepointbooks.com

Or follow me on BookBub to find out when I release new books!

www.ingramcontent.com/pod-product-compliance
Lightning Source LLC
Chambersburg PA
CBHW031257120726
47906CB00003B/785